The Beekeepers

The Peter Redgrove Library

Other Peter Redgrove books available from Stride:

The Peter Redgrove Library:
1. *In the Country of the Skin*
2. *The Terrors of Dr. Treviles*★
3. *The Glass Cottage*★
4. *The God of Glass*
5. *The Sleep of the Great Hypnotist*
6. *The Beekeepers*
7. *The Facilitators*
8. *The Colour of Radio: Essays and Interviews*
[★with Penelope Shuttle]

The Laborators
Abyssophone
Orchard End
What the Black Mirror Saw
Sheen
A Singer for the Silver Goddess

A Curious Architecture [contributor]
Earth Ascending [contributor]

i.m. Peter Redgrove:
Full of Star's Dreaming: Peter Redgrove 1932-2003

The Beekeepers

Peter Redgrove

Cover design by Neil Annat
Cover photos © Alistair Fitchett
Used with kind permission of the artist

The Peter Redgrove Library
is published by
Stride Publications
11 Sylvan Road, Exeter
Devon EX4 6EW
England

www.stridebooks.co.uk

Acknowledgements

Grateful acknowledgements are due to the National Theatre, whose
Platform Play commission in 1977 led to the devising of Matthew's
Magic Theatre; and to Giles Gordon, whose commission for *A Book of
Contemporary Nightmares* (Michael Joseph, London, 1977) helped evoke
Matthew and Guy's 'automatic script' as 'Our Lady of the Ice'.
The quotation on pages 37-38 is from Gerald Massey's *Ancient
Egypt, The Light of the World* (T. Fisher Unwin, London, 1907).

Thanks

The Peter Redgrove Library is grateful to the following subscribers who have helped make the publication of these titles possible:

Cliff Ashcroft
Andrew Bailey
Martin Bax
Hazel Carruthers
Philip Fried
Mark Goodwin & Nikki Clayton
David Grubb
Michael Longley
Adrian & Celia Mitchell
Brian Louis Pearce
Malcolm Ritchie
Geoff Sutton & Bernard Gilhooly
Leonie Whitton & David Westby

to the following for help, encouragement and support in other ways:

Tony Frazer
Neil Roberts
Penelope Shuttle
the late Philip Hobsbaum

and to Arts Council England, South West for financial support.

CONTENTS

Introduction

Mr Redgrove is a writer of morality plays: travelling around England with a wooden stage and a small cast of players, once a year he presents the ancient mysteries. But instead of the masks of saints and virgins, Redgrove's characters don the vestments of the shaman or the occultist and recite to us lessons of blood and primal sacrifice. *The Beekeepers* actually opens with a passage of automatic writing; a poet, Guy, falls into a light trance and becomes the medium for otherwise incommunicable truths: 'I did not make the bombs myself, though I took the terrorist handbook to Little Sean, as we call him . . .'

This message from the dead makes for a genuinely scary opening, and it sets the mood for a novel which, like a dowser's rod, shakes and shivers when it comes within the presence of invisible powers. It concerns two archetypal 'outsiders', Guy and Matthew, who, unable to cope with themselves or with others, become involved in divination as a way of re-ordering their lives. Their practices in white magic lead them into a precarious world, a world where the door between fantasy and reality has been left open – letting anything, literally anything, walk through. The conjurations of sex magic, and the unpredictable energies which such practices release, conspire to injure and destroy them. As the message had said at the beginning, 'I did not make the bombs myself . . .'

Magic of this kind is now a familiar component of some of the most interesting English writing. It is, after all, a way of describing certain social and political truths which remain undetected by the chic morality of conventional fiction. Many novelists are quite without beliefs of any kind, and revert to stylistic bravura or a kind of cynical objectivity. Magic, however, represents a coherent view of the world which can steady a writer's hand. In the occult, for example, Redgrove's interest in sexual politics and in the natural order find an appropriate home.

As a result, *The Beekeepers* is not a novel in any familiar sense. It is, rather, an examination, sometimes in didactic form, of certain kinds of occult practice – the bees of the title being the 'bird-flys', the souls of the dead, always fresh and always renewed. There is no great interest in plot or character as such – they are simply the wooden stage upon which the drama takes place. The emphasis of the novel lies in elucidating an idea, like coaxing a thread from a spider, which will in the end form a glittering net over the contemporary world.

There are certain dangers involved in this. The central idea has got to be a powerful one, and in this novel Redgrove sometimes reverts to melodrama in order to make his point. It also means that the major characters, Guy and Matthew, are on a fictional level incomplete.

They become representative figures, filled with strange powers and alien sensations which are more interesting than they themselves are. They are like the quartz digits on a Japanese watch – the intricate circuitry behind them cannot be seen, and has to be taken for granted.

The Beekeepers has the fire of theory in its head but, like any fire, it is sometimes difficult to discover the exact identity of the objects burning within it. And since the occult is still a somewhat marginal and little regarded area, the novel is filled with a kind of defiant rhetoric, an over-determined effort to be significant. As a result, it is filled with violence, madness, ghosts. And yet Redgrove's writing is powerful enough to make these spirits live, and *The Beekeepers* remains throughout an intriguing novel. Against all the odds it lives up to the claims which Redgrove obliquely makes for it: 'If some such "interpretations" were not given – and, indeed, within its limitations it might very well be correct – then the dream would vanish with all the other vapours of the night.' *The Beekeepers* is just such a work of interpretation; it reminds us that there are dreams and mysteries, and that to lose them would be to lose the most important part of ourselves.

Peter Ackroyd

Chapter one

A society of poets who have given up drink for mediumship

I

Under the lamplight the poet's fingers raced. 'This is a frightening one. Millie! Come quickly.' He swayed in his chair; the lids of his eyes were half-closed, showing the whites. 'Millie! Help me.' His body swayed stiffly, but his fingers holding the pencil sped across the big page like running water. Half the sheet was filled with close black writing; however fast the fingers moved, the characters kept their cohesion. Millie came into the circle of lamplight, but she did nothing. His head fell forward abruptly on his chest, but the fingers, with an independent life, continued writing. She folded her arms; a short sun-burnt woman with a strong face, dark-haired. Tears streamed from the poet's half-closed eyes and he was sobbing, yet the writing continued unperturbed. Still Millie did nothing. She stood there, brown-skinned and impassive like some anthropologist watching a native rite, forbidden by her science to intervene in the experiment. The great page of smooth white wallpaper was three-quarters black with writing now. With a quick sideways motion of the pencil to and fro, that left a big double line flourishing across the paper, the writing stopped. Millie immediately leaned forward and slid the paper away. The poet sat slumped and breathing in great shuddering gasps. She took his rigid head in her two hands and laid it gently back against the chair. The movement eased him; he sighed and relaxed a little, and his head turned from side to side. He murmured, like somebody coming out of a normal sleep; the eyes were fully closed now, but full of motion under the lids, like somebody surveying the remnant passages of a dream that was fading, then they opened slowly and he smiled at the woman standing there.

'Like a bad dream?' she asked.

'Very bad, it was very bad. I wish I had a drink.'

'I'll make you some tea.'

'That will have to do. I think I ought to read what happened.

Have you?'

'Not yet. I wanted to see that you woke without a stiff neck this time. You were like somebody having a heart-attack.' The round table on which the writing had been done was polished, and reflected the light like the surface of a well. 'I thought of your ghost rushing out of your mouth, gasping, and not being able to get back again.'

'Let me see what I wrote. Does it finish?'

She pulled up a chair and they read together, he still very pale, and his skin gleaming a little from sweat.

I did not make the bombs myself, though I took the terrorist handbook to Little Sean, as we call him. He made the bombs on the washstand, the marble-topped washstand. He pointed to my Mother's clock, the one with the four gilt pillars on the bedroom mantelpiece, that stood doubled in the mirror. 'It has a nice quiet tick,' Sean said, 'we could use that.' I pretended to be angry and flung myself on him: this was our game together. Our games at that time, when our Cause seemed so clear, always ended on the bed, and in it. Now the police are hunting us, we must ration our unconsciousness – no! I had forgotten, Sean's memory is so strong in me. He is dead. I shall be dead too, in exactly five and a half minutes, by my Mother's clock. I shall have made my revenge, on myself as well as on the others. Right and wrong will crash together in that instant.

I sit in the place of mirrors, with a small port and lemon on the iron table in front of me. Five minutes. 'You must jump into the centre of the whirlpool,' says Sean's memory, 'straight into the still eye of the storm. You carry the winds of the world and its lightning in the little knapsack I packed for you,' says dead Sean. 'It is your turn to jump into the wind that blows the souls away.'

In the four and three-quarter minutes left to me, if my Mother's clock does not fail me, I ponder the way my life has grown to this moment. I came into life, like all children, with the good and the bad entwined in my making. I have tried to separate them, but now after these minutes have passed they will be slammed into each other again. If these people drinking and laughing are evil, as we said, then it is right that I, in the name of the Cause, should kill them. But then it is wrong that I should die. If I am evil, it is right that I should die, but not right that these good happy people should die also. But in four minutes we shall all die together, all fused together in one death.

They say that when a person is drowning, all her life passes in front of her eyes. I am about to drown, but in fire. Pictures of my life pass in front of my eyes. The dead and the living walk, the good and the evil, the corpses and the quick, the meat and the eaters of meat.

Great blocks of clean glassy ice carried into the old shops. The Fishmonger's. The Butcher's. Mahon and Son, Quality Butchers. There was no 'Son'. Mr Mahon was my Father, and I his only child.

Sometimes I played in the shop during working-hours. They swept the sawdust off part of the floor and laid a blanket down on the tiles for me to play on, with my doll. I fed her and changed her and offered her tiny cuts of meat for her food, and I was very happy since I was with my Father. He was always busy with the meat and the joints and his regular customers. He and Michael, the butcher's boy, his apprentice, used to unhasp the great ice-storage room and swing open the doors thick as a white castle's. The bolt of these doors was a dull grey silver, and it was as long as I was tall. In came the ice-men with the blocks of ice as big as glass coffins. They wore sacking over their shoulders and sacking over their hands so that hefting the ice would not chap them. Michael and my Father would bring out the great headless open carcasses with their ribs showing like red and white piano keys and the fat as cold and firm as the marble counter they slapped the chops and steaks and giblets down on. With the saws and the cleavers the butcher and his boy would separate their Sunday joints for Mrs X and Mrs Y all buttoned up with their baskets on their arms and ready to discuss the price and the quality of the meat in the same tones as they dismembered their neighbours into juicy gossip-sized pieces. The small knives ease round the marbly knob and sever the tendons so that the joint comes free. What an atmosphere of satisfaction there was in the shopping of those days! Money was not plentiful, and it passed with deliberation. Value was visible; the source of the food and its quality was discussed with the shopkeeper. Especially the butcher, whose skill was displayed not only in his wielding of the knives, but in his conversation about his trade. He was the conversable watcher at the gates, the white cold gates. He sized up white and red death with its hollow ribs, he attacked it with his keen weapons, he cut it down to size and priced it, and the women converted it into Sunday luncheon.

13

The women were pleased to watch these men for their manliness in their blue and white striped aprons with the flap reaching to the breastbone where a startlingly white ivory button held its upper portion in place in case of blood that splashed. You could watch the meat and the sinews work in their bare forearms below the rolled-up sleeves as they expertly sawed and sliced and jointed the cold carcasses. With much jovial talk they would do it, their punctuation the chunk of the cleaver into the meat and the wooden block under it, and then the slap of the flesh on the grease-proof paper swung by the corners on to the scales: 'That will be three-and-sixpence, Mrs V and thank you very much indeed.' And the men loved to show off their mastery of meat, how they dealt dismemberment with a jest and a wink amid the bloody sawdust, how (the women might secretly imagine) they dealt with all meat, living or dead in some such manner; though if it were alive they would have left their knives in their racks in the closed and dark shop, and this is how at night, in the bedroom, they swung the girls into bed despite all protests, in a flow of jovial patter, this is how they arranged them on the sheets, all limp with no-resistance, this dead, relaxed flopping was the outcome of their strenuous manly love, all passion spent, the little death, the poor maiden a mere love's carcass, to be done with as they wished. Even as a little girl I could feel the way men and women were united in that shop, and how they got their satisfactions out of their teasing jokes, and their gossip, and their mouth-waterings of the meat. In those days shopping was like street-theatre, with a cast of heroes and heroines, dragons to be cut up and eaten, ugly sisters and comedians to take the piss out of everything. No wonder we loved the pantomimes at Christmas! That spirit has gone, killed by the luxurious television images. Now we make gods of the living dead of the white screens. In the realms of the dead, whether it is behind the marble stone or the marble screen that lights up or within the stone skull of memory, it is the bad currency that drives out the good. 'We in the Cause have real dead for our heroes,' Sean's memory tells me, 'and you, my dear, have three minutes only of this unreal pub-life left to you before you are really dead at last.'

My stepmother's name was Jessie. We were not close. I was eleven. I still loved to play with my doll in the butcher's shop, and my Father promised me I should soon have an apron and I would be allowed to play at serving the customers. For now I was to play in my part of the shop with my doll so that I should not get my dress stained. Michael was taking some hearts in a tray out of the shop. A piece of fat or something of the kind had fallen on the floor. Michael stepped on it and slipped and dropped the tray of hearts near where I was playing with my doll. One of the hearts landed very near me and split and some residual blood in it splashed my frock. I lifted my skirt to see if the stain had come through and I found blood on my pants. I heard my Father in the shop slicing some carcass with a great thunk and crying out with laughter. I heard answering laughter from a customer and the rattling of money. I stood up. The blood was running down my legs and I called out to my Father that I had cut myself and that it was under my skirt and that he was to come please and help me. I saw his head jerk round and then he looked back to stick the edge of the cleaver in the great wooden block. Then he came quickly towards me. There was blood on his hands and I could see it on the white stripes of his apron. He lifted me up and told me to hush and Michael to mind the shop. He carried me down the street past the houses, there was blood on my skirt and on his apron and he carried me like an infant but I was content with that, and the blood was still trickling down my legs. He rapped on the door and my stepmother opened it and went pale but he said, 'It's all right. Maureen is a woman now.' Her hand went up to her mouth and the words seemed to make no sense to her. She took me from my Father and she had a cross look on her face. I remember the police constable was sitting at the table drinking tea. I looked down at the blood on me and I wanted to kiss my Father but the door was empty and he had gone back to the shop. My stepmother took me into the little bathroom next to the kitchen and made me take my pants down. I saw her looking at me strangely, then suddenly her hand whipped out and she slapped my face and I found I was crying. I can hear her voice hissing now, like her name, Jessie: 'Slut,' her memory hisses at me, 'little witch, you are too young to be a woman.'

Blood and ice. The ice-men lifted the blocks out of their van with great tongs that bit into the sides. The largest blocks, such as those brought for my Father's ice-room, they slid, in the grip of those tongs, down a plank on to a little trolley. In the sunlight the ice slid along that plank in its own juice. Sullivan, T. P. Sullivan: that was the name of the fish-monger. I cannot remember him, but I remember the wide-open golden eyes of the fish he sold, and their sheer silver bodies; the streamlined food. They said these silvery messengers were good brain-food, the flaky flesh, the watery blood. I saw the body of the young man killed in the quarry explosion lying on sacking in the outhouse. Michael's teenage son and I had taken a dare and crawled into the little outhouse mortuary through a loose plank. He was a devil, that little Jacob, he swept the sheet off the poor young man and there he was, naked, and that was the first time I had seen what a man keeps between his legs. Thank God it's different on a living man, but corpses have little pricks that have retired into themselves, particularly if their death is frightful. This was like a little flesh bud or tuber in a nest of black hairs stark as twigs on the bloodless skin, and Jacob swung his torch near it so that it grew an enormous shadow over the wooden wall. Then he switched his torch out. I heard him creeping about, and then suddenly a horrible bright face with closed eyes and a down-turned mouth appeared about six feet from me. Jacob, the little bugger, had crept up to the corpse and put his torch under its chin and turned it on so that the dead face should grimace at me with all its shadows cast upwards. There was a click and it went dark, but with another click the death-mask of Jacob hung in the room and swung laughing hollowly towards me. I kept my nerve enough to snatch the torch from Jacob for I knew that it was his face. He saw that he had gone far enough and he did not tease me any more. I wanted to look at the corpse and wanted to show brave. I examined it in the torch beam: the face was very peaceful and composed, the mouth a little turned down as though from a mildly disturbing dream, but the poor body had great rents in it and I could see the creamy bone of the ribs through one large flap that was hanging loose at his side. They looked like big red and white piano keys. On his chest over his heart there was a great inky bruise. I saw how a man could become in a flash meat like the carcasses in my Father's shop, but those carcasses were all headless. I could not place that man's calm dreaming face on the neck of this carcass though it was plainly there, in front of me. It did not belong there, but it was there. It was life dreaming and death supine and the two were joined together with the neck of a man. I wanted to take that handsome face with me, I wanted it for my own. I wanted to separate it from its death, from its ragged carcass. He was so alive, though sleeping, in his face, that it might at any moment have opened its eyes and its dead lips and talked to me, but I knew, at the same time, from the torn body, that it never could. That head rode its monstrous carcass. *If only it could fly free, away from this dark shed. I touched a cheek of the head, it was cold. I touched the chest, on the unbruised side, it was cold. Then I touched the cock, it was cold and it was firm and gristly and rounded and neat, like a purse. The two balls were hard and cool in their bag of skin which slid over its contents to the pressure of my fingers as the pimpled skin of a goose from the ice-room is loose and firm over the meat after it has been plucked. I wanted to take this too, as a trophy, as a secret I could keep for myself. I looked back at Jacob: my seriousness had frightened him, he wanted to leave now. The corpse lay on sacking; I pulled this up and saw the big blocks of ice on which it rested. I probed them with the beam of my torch, and the light shifted and glistened among the bubbles and cracks, tracks and fanned strains in the water, like glass books with thin cracked white pages of glass and sentences of glass written on them. Jacob took the torch from me and dropped the sacking and we put the sheet back over the corpse, and he led the way out through the broken wall. Two and a half minutes to go.*

II

The poet, Guy, was not married to his Millie. She would not have him; she was glad that they lived together, but they had agreed that marriage, secular or sacerdotal, was not for them. Guy was still married, but elsewhere. His wife had left him, with their two children, when, in his cups, he had lashed out at her for mocking his poetry and his drinking. He felt that she had waited until he was really drunk before abusing him, risking what might come of injury, and in that gamble taking as a prize bodily harm only sufficient to brand him as a brute: the one blow that landed. Millie had a degree in psychology from Reading — this was experimental psychology and had, she said, taught her nothing about her mind or anybody else's, with the exception of those of experimental psychologists, and what they would consider evidence. She was not a medium, or a poet, or any kind of writer; she was an observer, rather brutally so, an intellectual, a withholder of judgment. She would give her body for pleasure, an observable phenomenon, but she never used the word 'love'. Experimental

17

psychology had had an effect, then. Yet she stayed with Guy, and felt like a one-woman safari in the wilderness of his mind. It was to be her territory; one day, when she had either cleared it and settled it, or understood it, she might love it.

The two had met at a poetry-reading at the University. Millie had been persuaded to come by friends. They made her read some of Guy's poetry beforehand, and even persuaded her to compose a vote of thanks in advance — it would give her a chance of hitting back if she felt like it, they said. She said she was not interested in poetry, but came all the same. She found herself interested in the poet, who was a tall and burly man with a full beard and a domed bald forehead. He was dressed in a roll-necked sweater and a very wrinkled leather coat; the leather seemed stiff and old and in need of a clean and on the point of cracking where the elbows bent. He had a strong, clear voice, and he had been drinking. One knew this not because he was swaying or speaking indistinctly, but because his timing was out. He introduced the poems with a rush of associations, and these were somewhat more difficult to understand than the poems they were supposed to clarify; then he would pause for effect, which turned to a pause for reflection, which went on long enough for him to feel he needed to change the subject, and this added to his listeners' difficulties. Millie wondered why he should drink so much, if a poet was anything but another name for a drunkard. She could recall three of the poems and their introductions quite clearly. She had the poems by heart; the spiel she remembered was a construct, an analogue; in the interests of science not too much altered. She said it was science, and not love, that helped her remember.

'I'm going to read three short bee-poems. Bees are very important. There are legends, but they make you interested in bees without explaining anything. Virgil's bees were spontaneously created from the body of a two-year-old calf whose apertures had all been sealed, and which had been beaten to death with clubs. Out of the strong came forth sweetness: as though the animal, giving up its great big life, made many tiny perfect winged souls. Sweetness and light . . . the beautiful whispering beeswax candle and the honey that will temper sharp wine . . . the candle made of sections of comb marked with its hexagonal cells, rolled into a cone round a wick . . . shedding light and whispering, it is said, with the voices of the dead on winter evenings.

'The dead are involved in it, you know. The moon is the hive, and the stars her bees. In Virgil's vision of the underworld, the humming reincarnating dead played and sported like swarming bees. There were three nymphs called Thriae, who fed on honeycomb. After eating it they told the truth, but if they got no honey they told lies. "But this infinite Hive of honey, this insatiable whirlpoole of the covetous mind, no Anatomy, no dissection hath discovered to us . . . "Quite a lot of you are scientists, aren't you? I can see you saying, "Why doesn't he keep to the point?" But not keeping to it, is the point. You need poets to remind you of what you keep on forgetting by keeping to the point. It's a difficult profession, because it's often what the poet prefers to forget too. But the thoughts swarm like bees, and cluster round a theme. However sharp, however stinging the individual thoughts, they work together and give pleasure. The rich honey-smell, the rich hum. Dante saw the souls of the blessed feeding on the great petals of paradise. And their song was a bee-song, made of many hymns. There is a psychological type called "introverted intuitive". Most of you are "extrovert intellect-sensation" types. The hive needs us all. We poets are like the despised drones. You may not like us, but we scatter our seed, and the Queens are fertilised. Most of us die after a short flight. I'd better give you a poem. I want to compare some winged beasties. I think of wasps as the flip side of bees, and flies the black shadow of the spinning coin. I call my poem "Details":

'Wasps in black clouds scudding against an angry sun
Their wings fan a special venomous storm

Eyes like cobbles in rain, convulsions in the tail,
Winged transistors of cellophane and functional liquors

Broadcasting news of rebellion in Doppler snarls;
The fly concurs, black medical bag full of diseases.

The bee is not moved, continues chewing down its flower
Like a winged bear, much travelled, with dusty nap,

Trousers full of waxy pollen, chewer and spitter
Of hexagonal mansions brimming with amber,

Manufacturer of whispering wax and energetic sweetness.

'They're so *handsome*, you see! Why were the priestesses of
the Delphic oracle called "Melissai" — bees? In Renaissance
art, the foetus in the womb was thought of as being built as the
honeycomb by bees: that is why bees attend Venus in Cranach's
painting. You know that humming *Om* like a hive calms you and
brings you visions. Have you thought of doing a study of dreams
produced under control conditions, and those produced after the
ingestion of mead? Over a dinner-table lighted by beeswax candles,
you will find the skin easier, more erotic. The bees gathered that
nectar from the flowers in their honey-stomachs, and since the
hive needed no more added to its stores, that nectar turned to
wax in the bee, and the forager turned builder of honey-cells.
And the flowers gathered that nectar from the sun and the sun's
light, distilling it through the day. And now your loose-clothed
skins drink that light stored in the candles and become seduced
— scientists, the negative ions given off by the candles into the
air are measurable! Experiment! Learn to see visions as you make
love in bed: the bees will help you.
  'I'd better read another poem. This is about the great collegiate
church Glasney, which flourished in the Middle Ages at the head
of the Penryn River in Cornwall. It was equal to Glastonbury
at the height of its fame, and was as savagely reduced, almost
the first of the monasteries to suffer so. In the indictment they
were blamed for their hobby-horses and other pagan festivals.
The abbey was founded by Bishop Bronescombe, who was told
in a dream to look for bees swarming on a willow by a spring. I
have been to Glasney. The spring is still there, and some stones.
The mud of the spring is very cooling. I saw no bees there, but
I could imagine the hum of the chant of the many choirs in the
tall cool church, all gone now. You can hear a kind of humming

in old churches sometimes, like a wire stretched in the wind. It is behind hearing, but it accompanies prayers. It's God's telephone exchange: an exchange clicks and hums in its many particles, switches and cells. There's a number telephone engineers know that will get you through anywhere. I think the bees know it. This poem is called "Glasney":

'The thin clear stream
Flashing behind the dead tree shaped
Like a skeleton with a rippling ghost in it;
Thigh-deep in the mire, a willow
Purring with the swarm of bees like grapes hanging.
The wind of the other world came through this spring,
The bees arranged in it like a honey slipstream.
The bishop knew where to build by bees and mire.

There is a pagan cellar beneath this church
Solid with beeswax.

The ancient hives perfume the modern building.
This is a secret; the hives are secret churches;

Good people are turned to bees and honey when they die;
There are so many journeys to be made from grave to flower,

So much wax to be packed into luminous dwellings
For ghosts in filmy wings brushed with rummaged pollen
To dwell in with the queen in that hum of perfection.

'I see it's nearly time to finish. My last poem is more about wax than about bees. Besides their being introverted intuitives, poets are often said to be effeminate.'

At this the big burly man with the thick beard squared up and looked round his audience with such a pugilistic attitude, and with such an innocent stare under his bald brow, that everybody laughed rather happily. The poet smiled.

'Yes, that's right. It's an amusing thought. A lot of my imagery comes from enthusiastic touch and texture. My skin is very erotic. The books tell me that this is more usual in women. In men, when it exists, the feeling increases with age. I love getting wet, and smearing interesting things on my skin. You may think that's mad. Of course it is. Hands up people who like getting wet in a warm summer shower.'

Almost everybody's hand went up.

'Who likes rolling in a muddy field?'

Two hands went up, wavered, and went down again.

'Not many. Well, I can tell you, there's a zing about it. Outrageousness sharpens the senses. These are very minor liberties taken with one's person. There are worse things to do that bring life also. Murder, and the thought of murder. Christian religion is founded on that gory mystery, the Jesus-murder. Blood is shed in Voodoo and other possession-cults. The dead flock to it, in their swarms. In Voodoo you can drink a nasty alcohol in which something has been pickled. This small outrage opens the senses too. The mind's playtime. Let it run everywhere, like hot wax. I call this one "Room of Wax"!

'The witch pulled the lever and her cellar filled with hot wax,
The mice, the boxes of nails, the live matches,
The well-head, the altar and the human sacrifice:
The girl with the welling heart, and the goat-headed man
With dagger dripping on the return-stroke —
Before they knew it, in a flash-flood
Of hardening wax of bees, caught for ever in the act.
The carpet made of her friend's skin, "Is it not better
To remember him?" The small pizzle lank and empty.

She would walk over it barefoot, remembering him.
It is like brown suede, we make love on it. On the shelf
The young black cat sat in the jar pickling
A smoky wine: "If you want to be a witch you must drink it."
I did, and I am; the cellar door swinging open on the smooth
        wax room,
The secrets running away like water in the blueflare blowflame.'

The poet stopped, looked round him, and sat down. He cleared his throat and obviously wanted something to drink. The chairman fussily started pouring him a glass of water from a dusty carafe, and said, 'I call upon Ms Er to propose a vote of thanks.' Ms Er, who was scribbling on a piece of paper, started. She rose slowly to her feet.

'It's my happy task to propose a vote of thanks. I suppose I am one of those extroverted sensation-intellect types our poet mentioned. I've experienced several sensations while I have been listening, not all of them pleasant.' The poet seemed about to interrupt. 'No, I'm not being rude about this. I'm quite sure that he meant to stroke our fur the wrong way sometimes, and it is a fact that I felt that prickle of hair on the shoulders which is said to accompany good poetry, like the passing of a ghost in front of one's face.' The poet looked interested, and bent forward as if he saw the speaker plainly for the first time. It was Millie.

'Our poet may be introverted intuitive, and he's haptic as well: this is his sense of touch. Obviously his mind is bombarded with sensory input, and for most of us it has survival value to ignore the greater proportion of this: we have evolved because certain characteristics, including a receptivity that would hold us spellbound and helpless with sensed detail, have been bred out of us. It has been said that the matriarchal, poetical, pious Neanderthal sub-species of humanity were lingerers in sensory detail and the Cro-Magnon were sterner and harder, and won the evolution stakes. Our poet has plunged us in this making stream tonight. He has drawn our conscious minds closer to our subliminal perceptions: the two in him must be very close by nature.

> 'Ha' you felt the wooll o' the Bever?
>   Or Swans Downe ever?
> Or have smelt o'the bud o'the Brier?
>   Or the Nard in the fire?
> Or have tasted the bag of the Bee? . . .

'Well, we have through his poetry, and I ask you to express your thanks in the usual way.'

The applause was of decent volume, if it lasted for rather short a time. People were anxious to get away, either because they'd had enough, or they were thirsty, hungry or had to catch trains. There was a general exodus, and Guy, caught up with the chairman, was not able to do what he wanted, which was to meet this girl who must have gone to the trouble of reading his work beforehand and working out a speech. The chairman, an elderly Eng. Lit. lecturer, had been explaining that they did not usually get time for questions, and Guy was telling him that that was the best time as far as he was concerned, since he enjoyed improvising. 'Weren't you improvising as you talked?' asked the chairman. 'No,' said Guy, 'that was more like divination. I can't work out what these poems mean sometimes; though I knew when I wrote them. It doesn't make me a bad person though,' as he watched the shade of disapproval cross the man's face. They were now in the aisle opposite the row of seats from which Millie had spoken. Guy noticed a piece of paper on the flattened writing-arm of her chair. He darted in and picked it up. It was a ball-point drawing of somebody with great hunched shoulders and a streaked beard, with a turned-down mouth and dark shadows on his face. He was dressed in the skin of a cow, and his head was bare, tall and pointed. Guy turned round to see the chairman waiting. 'Shall we go to the students' pub?' 'I've found a portrait of the Abominable Snowman,' said Guy; 'I had no idea that your students had such delicacy of feeling.'

III

'He led the way out through the broken wall.' Guy gazed at the script, black and closely set on the large page. He propped it up on the kitchen counter, against the bread-bin. 'Great blocks of clean ice carried into the old shops.' He savoured the phrases. 'Millie, this is not like the usual stuff.'

'You have to accept that it could have been done by a sub-personality of yourself.'

'Of course I accept that. I would even say that it's a part of myself split off when I stopped drinking. Call it my anima.'

'Your anima a mad Irish bomber?'

'No, of course not. But the psyche employs symbols, and it doesn't mind about space and time. Ireland is split into warring factions. It has a religious war. Once it believed that there was no original sin; that life was innocent. That was the native religion. The Christian church would not have the synthesis. Alas, to these believers either the world is lyrical and sinless or it is solid sin, to be purged in a bomb-flash.'

'Guy, I'm worried. If this is like a dream that you are having, might it not mean that you have something so bottled up in you that it resembles the train of a bomb laid, a stroke, madness, something like that?'

'We agreed that boozing as I did was to quieten something in me that needed to speak. We said we'd let it speak. If I drop dead, then that's part of it. I don't want to, but there it is. It's the kind of thing that can happen anyway in middle age.' Guy began to mix his honey-and-water.

Millie was at the phone. She was speaking excitedly. 'It's Matthew! He wants to come over from the Institute. He's got something to show us.'

'Well, let him come, it's about time. Soon as he likes.'

Matthew was the second member of their society of two. A year ago, both men had agreed to give up drink, come what may. Matthew was the heavier drinker, and nearly ten years older than Guy, which made changing a habit like drinking a big commitment. Both men were afraid of DTs. Matthew had at last experienced them after a long bout, and the description had frightened Guy. It was green insects. Matthew had woken up in the small hours. His eyes snapped open and he was fully awake in that instant, with a full recall of the last two days' boozing, the sleazy little club after closing-time, the whiskies at a pound a throw, and the woman who had sat down with him drinking whatever they had brought to her for his pound, until his money was gone. Some irrational Providence prevented him from spending his fare home, and he saw himself weaving home from the local station staggering from side to side of the pavement, as though he were watching a film. Now, fully awake at something like four o'clock, without a drink in the flat, and the bedside lamp still on, he reached out for his cigarettes — and drew his hand back with a yelp. On the bedside table, in the place of the packet and the matches, was a large green insect, about the size of a dictionary, staring at him with cobbled eyes and slowly-champing jaws. He knew he was not still drunk — he had never felt more sober — but still it champed, and he could see it in exact focus even without his glasses. The antennae were curved and squat, rather like a series of green buttons fastened together. He looked up at the ceiling, and it was studded with green insects of various sizes, moving slowly with deliberate steps, lifting their sappy green legs one after another. As he watched, he saw that some of these bugs were moulting. They scraped at their heads until their skin came free, and pushed the loose helmet forward with their fore-limbs. The rest of the carapace came with it, as a man might pull off a stiff cream shirt over his head, or climb out of a suit of fibreglass armour. The bug underneath was of a more superbly vivid green. The husks began to fall like feathers, and the room's air was full of them, like a pillow-fight. On the bedside table, the first green creature was standing, as it were, beside itself: it had separated from its moult, which stood at its side like a white shadow. Matthew pulled at the pillow with some idea of smashing the insects, but it came apart in his hands in a shower of green bugs flying upwards with brilliant green wings leaving behind them their empty husks, which showered like big scurf over the bed. Now Matthew felt the bed heaving in a mouldy way as though it was coming apart, and he realised that it too was made of green beetles that were moulting. As he struggled to get up from it his leg went right into the mass of insects. He said that he felt distressed to think that he might be treading on any of them before they could free themselves from their old skins, since the new bodies were so beautiful and so utterly green. The whirling bodies filled his head and as he lost consciousness he saw that his finger-joints were loosening and brilliant green bugs were shooting from his fingertips.

When he woke again he was lying on his bed, as he should have been. The room was full of green light from the fluorescent street-lamps, and the bedside light was off. He reached for his cigarettes, and then his watch. It was six o'clock. The whisky was coming out of him in big rolling drops all over his body, and he was trembling.

He distrusted doctors and hospitals profoundly, but this was a special occasion. There was obviously something very wrong, even though its cause was plain enough, being clear, amber, spirituous and completely irresistible. At the out-patients department they checked his urine and his blood, and one of the Pakistani doctors listened to his chest and palpated his abdomen. There was much clucking and shaking of heads when he told them his story, and a nurse came in with two large capsules which he was induced to take with some water. 'Why should I take these?' he cried, and they pointed to his trembling hands. They asked him to undress, gave him some faded, roughly-washed, unironed pyjamas, and led him to a high hospital bed of white-painted iron.

In the morning there were two more capsules, and a breakfast of strong tea and remarkably good fried bacon. This time the doctor who came to examine him was white and grey, white skin, grey hair, grey suit, white coat, and trailed behind him a gaggle of much younger people, boys and girls almost, who seemed to Matthew, who had been a schoolmaster, like sixth-formers. The senior doctor allowed one of the girls to examine Matthew, and then one of the boys. There was rapid murmuring in medical pig-latin, too fast for Matthew to catch anything but the word 'ascites' repeated several times. Nobody looked him in the eye. When they had finished, the sheet was thrown over him, and the company of doctors and semi-doctors walked away to the next bed, which had been screened off. Matthew felt no sense of outrage — that was something in the pills, he thought. 'Am I all right?' he said to the nurse who came to tuck in the disturbed bedding.

'Yes, you are,' she said. 'Doctor says you are in good shape, everything considered. They want you to tell your nasty dream to another doctor this afternoon.'

'A psychiatrist?'

'A psychiatrist,' she agreed.

'Well, I might,' he said, and fell asleep.

There were two psychiatrists, not one, in the little office with the long couch. Matthew made for the couch, but was asked to sit down in an ordinary chair in front of a desk, where the younger of the two men was seated: a nondescript doctor-type with a lean chin and greased hair. The other man sat by the window, and was rather difficult to see distinctly in the afternoon light, which threw his shadow into the room. Matthew could see a big nose and combed-back long white hair: the man appeared to be about seventy. The younger man said, 'I hear you've had a nightmare.'

Matthew told his story, and felt himself trembling as again the pillow burst into bugs and his fingernails seemed to fly. The doctor in front of him listened without comment. When Matthew had finished, he said, 'I think you know that this means you must stop drinking. I can give you some capsules to help you.'

'They won't satisfy, will they?'

'Drink will send you mad, you know. You have to face up to that. It will probably send you mad before it kills your body.'

'Well, it could hardly do it the other way, could it?' The phrase 'a mad ghost' came into Matthew's mind, with an impression of fleece-like whirling skins, human ones this time, and empty, but with the eye-skin still under the lids, and showing faded irises of blue and brown in the white whirl. He felt a crawling of his own skin, like the dabbing of weak fingers.

'We're doing our best to help. If you take the pills, to make you calmer, and the capsules, to counteract the effect of the alcohol, I'd be happy to see you here from time to time. We can discuss your problems.'

'Are you sure they are quite distinct from your problems? Some of us become doctors, some of us drunks.'

'It's you we have to talk about. I don't want you to go downhill any further.'

'I don't want to be rude, but doctors are pretty low in my estimation.'

'Is it your anger which makes you drink?'

'Oh, shit,' said Matthew, and got up to leave.

'Think of *bees*,' said a deep voice from the window. Matthew wanted to listen to this voice, and he sat down again. The older man leaned forward into the room. His voice was very relaxed and resonant. His face was smooth and rather grey, like an old woman's, but it was not sexless as Matthew would have expected. The eyes were bright and looked mischievous, regarding him slightly sideways: with desire, as Matthew realised with a slight shock. He felt he didn't want too much of that gaze; it was embarrassing to be given the eye by an old man at his age.

'Why . . . ?' said Matthew.

'Why nothing,' said the deep voice; 'just think of bees.'

IV

It was a simple enough idea: think of bees. The speaker had been impressive and sure of himself. That had given Matthew a direction, like a magnetism. He thought of the iron filings in the school experiment suddenly aligning on the sheet of white paper when the magnet came near, making their swirls, the forces in the air around the iron revealed. Matthew resented authority, but not this magnetism. It was like a current produced in himself by the approach of a stronger field. It was not like an imposed educative plan. The iron filings wheeled and returned to the north and south poles of the magnet — like bees returning to the hive, black bees on a white sky. He saw this, like a sudden snapshot, as the thought entered his mind. He remembered dipping a magnet in the box of filings at school, how they clung, and how difficult it was to get the magnet clean afterwards. They hung in clustered matted streaks, clinging to each other — indeed, just like bees that swarm. He remembered throwing a pinch of the filings in the fire — they sparkled like flying stars.

At the pub that evening, with his second whisky, a double, naturally, in his glass (the first whisky was an emergency treatment taken without reflection) he began to muse on the beautiful amber colour, and the meaning of the word 'spirit'. How marvellous it was that one made grain decay, deliberately and with great finesse, and then distilled it to obtain 'spirit' that rallied and then killed the 'spirit' in a man. That beautiful tawny colour was the shade of ripe wheat. He took another sip: the whisky ramped down his gullet, he imagined, like a lion that spread light as it roared back at the darkness within. 'There's a poem there,' thought Matthew, and then, 'out of the strong came forth sweetness,' and he thought again of bees, Samson's bees, the answer to the riddle, life and energy distilled from the body of a dead lion.

'Am I getting these thoughts from the hospital capsules? If so, they will save me money, as I already feel quite mellow. I'll try a single,' rising for his third whisky.

Matthew had been a schoolmaster for the LCC, but had applied for early retirement, and got it. He now lived on his small pension, and his writing. He reviewed a little, and he published poetry. His verse was usually jokey, and full of word-play; sprightly was the word.

PLATALOW'S BUNG

She is a memorial to the idea of the bungalow;
Plato's Bungalow, the bungalow with the name-plate
For the postman, 'Plato'. I asked him, is that a name
Or are the people there called 'Plato'. 'Oh yes,' he said,
'That is the bungalow of the Plato family: Jim Plato,
Shirley Plato, and little Lettice Plato, and they call their dog . . .'
'Don't tell me,' I said, 'they call it "Socrates",'
'No, as a matter of fact, it bit me the other day,
So I know its name, the brute is called "Diana", it
Drew blood.' 'Thank you, postman, so that I shall know
You again, you are Mr — Actaeon?' 'No, Lord
Love you, Sir! not at all, my name's Ed; Ed, Sir,
Ed Imion, and my mother was Greek.'

His deeper poetic vein was old age. He was terrified of growing old; and now, rather abruptly it seemed, he was sitting in a pub, aged fifty-seven, and feeling like a twelve-year-old after his encounter with the doctors. Twelve: perhaps that was his true age; 'I wonder if I've ever felt older than twelve?' he said aloud, and then looked round to see if anyone had heard. There was nobody sitting with him; his sudden remark to himself had gone unnoticed. It wouldn't really have mattered if it had not. He thought of his son John who had died when he was twelve. Was it that which broke up the marriage and started the drinking? So long ago, nearly twenty-five years. He looked at the palm of his hand; it was marked with the black ink he used for his poems. Sometimes he put down his pen and touched his brow in thought, and occasionally the ink would get there, and he would wear it all day until somebody pointed it out to him. He had once seen a colour photograph of the corpse of an old woman; her whole face below the sunken eyes was covered with a mask of black mould, like a domino falling below her throat and brushing the dusty white nightie she wore. The thought disturbed him, and he realised that it had jumped into his mind and made him forget that he had just got up and crossed to the bar for his fourth drink, whose amber colour he was now considering in its glass. How like honey it was, he thought, in colour anyway, as he put it to his lips, and there is a sweetness in the fire: sweetness and light, he thought, sweetness and light. There was a kind of click in his head, and the room came into clearer focus. He went back over his conversation with the doctors, and indeed the whole experience of DTs, and it now seemed most poetic and not at all frightening. After all, there was great energy in that vision of the bugs; the only thing wrong with them was that they were all doing different things, all about their own concerns. Perhaps on their next moult they would become bees, he thought, and laughed aloud. As he got up to fetch another whisky he found that his legs had gone rubbery, so he sat down again and lit a cigarette. At almost the same moment he felt a sharp pain in his hand, and he looked at where the cigarette had burnt down and was scorching his fore and second finger. 'I must have blacked out a moment,' he said, brushing his hands together. There was ash all over the front of his trousers, and he wanted to piss, but he didn't yet trust his legs. The clarity had gone. 'I must be getting old,' he said quietly, and thought of one of his poems that now seemed not about himself, but about the old doctor who had taught him to think about bees. 'That is a way to get old,' he said, and had a quick picture of himself sitting there, inky, covered with ash, and not able to walk. His poem drew again into his mind, and it was not words he saw or heard, but the old doctor again: 'Bee-doctor; bee-keeper; does he keep bees I wonder, so he can think of them all day?'

EARTH

By the hearth,
The discomfort of earth, time's fire,
Withers him. He shrinks
Into his eyes, which well and gleam,
Glitter with sleep, sink shut,
Fed by the dry runnels of his face.
The old apple shrivels, but,
For a while, the smell is sweet as blossom,
And the skin soft as warm flowers,
For, as I disturb his sleep, and rise to go,
This goodness wells from the warm eyes
Along the runnels, creating the face:
And as his eyes open and the world returns
So the wrinkles flood over his face
Like earth irrigated with kindliness.

The picture faded. Matthew felt warm tears running down his face and splashing off his chin. He snuffled and searched for a hankie. He hadn't got one. 'Oh my God, whisky-tears. Those bloody capsules and those doctors. How am I to get home?' He suddenly noticed that his friend Guy was bending over him, looking concerned. He had come in for some drinking, hoping to find Matthew. 'It's no good, Guy, I've gone all queer. I've got to get home. Get us a quarter-bottle at the bar, there's a good chap, and take me home?' That had been a year ago.

V

A year later Millie was at the phone, speaking excitedly. Guy was mixing a glass of honey and hot water, which he found reviving after he had finished a trance-session, and which helped his cough.

'It's Matthew! He wants to come over from the Institute. He's got something to show us.'

'Well, let him come, it's about time. Soon as he likes.'

They were back in the sitting-room, and Millie was re-reading Guy's automatic script. The bell rang, and Guy got up to let Matthew in. He looked white and huddled in his old overcoat. For a moment Guy thought he had gone back on the bottle, but then Matthew took a roll of stiff wallpaper from the big poacher's pocket where he used to secrete whisky-bottles when they drank sitting in the cinema, between opening-times. He unrolled the paper, and showed that it was covered with close black marks. They spread it over the polished table, and began to read.

Sean walked out of the post office doorway carrying the transistor into the sunlight and there was a sudden sharp bang and a spurt of flame. I could not see in the smoke but there was a photographer there and his picture showed the stump of my lover's wrist all glistening in the instant before the blood leapt out of it after the bomb in the transistor case had blown the hand off. He died as he lay, his blood spread over the marble steps and his face half in it with his eyes wide open as though he were watching himself die in a mirror of his own blood. I could not understand why he did not leave our bomb in the post office, as we had arranged. In the photograph, which I have with me now, his face looked stupid with shock, as if the master in our school those years ago had asked him a too-difficult question. He looked so at a loss that it made me laugh; I could not connect that poor stump of his wrist with that comical expression on his face. And now that little voice comes into my head again and says, 'Stumped for an answer, my love,' and 'two minutes to go.'

That voice is the voice of the little snaking contradictions, the spirit of contradiction, the ancient serpent twining his way in and out of life, dissolving the boundaries between people, dissolving the bound-

aries between good and bad, bringing it all back to one thing. I was in church and they were saying how the Christ child was born from a stainless virgin. The little serpent voice wriggled its way in and told me a riddle: 'Who had a baby without sex?' That was easy: 'The Virgin Mary,' I said. It was a catechism from the little blood-red serpent. Then it asked: 'Who had sex without having a baby?' That was easy too: 'I did,' I replied.

Perhaps it is the voice of Sean's child. My period is almost late, and I could be carrying Sean's child. If I am, it has one and three-quarter minutes to be unborn in. Perhaps Sean's child is speaking on behalf of all the children not yet born in this mirrored room. That girl over there with the blue headscarf is very pregnant; she should not be smoking. It will make no difference now. How many of these women are carrying children at all their stages of growth? How many invisible children are there in this smoky room of mirrors who speak through my serpent voice and in my serpent actions their request not to be born into this violent world where good preys on evil? For this voice sees both sides of every question, and is never stumped for an answer. It simply takes the opposite side. If I weep for our martyrs, it cracks a little joke. If I am happy and want to share life in the happy pub, it makes sure I take our knapsack-bomb with me, primed to explode in one and a half minutes now. This will be the sharpest contradiction of all.

The English soldiers held their parade today, poor young men, born to die, birth-wet behind the ears and shining with spit and polish. I saw them in their best uniforms with faces bright as buttons, the stern military expression stamped there like the coat of arms on bright brass. They rattled and banged their rifles and slammed their hands on the polished rifle butts, and they slammed the butts down by their highly-waxed boots, and they slammed those mirror-boots down on the parade-ground asphalt to show they were not afraid of whatever bones and ghosts lay beneath the resounding soil. There was a brass band making a brave sound, and none of it to do with killing. They marched out of their barracks like a carpet of identical gleaming ants, all shining with birth-juices, fresh out of the egg. The corporal reported to the sergeant-major, and the sergeant-major reported to the duty officer, and the duty officer reported to the commanding officer, all like honest dogs barking on the clear morning air. Then there was firing in the distance and a siren on the barracks roof and the carpet of ants unwove itself back into the barracks and soon after the big doors swung open and the armoured cars spun out revving, accelerated away. Soon there was more firing. The chocolate soldiers had turned in a flash to soldiers of blood. The cruel pantomime had escaped into the audience from its lighted stage.

I saw the men carrying the boy back to his home. They had him on a door torn by some bomb from its hinges, and they held it on their shoulders. Their faces looked as drilled as the soldiers' faces, drilled and willed. In their grief, God forgive me, I saw pleasure. I saw their enjoyment in their stern roles that knew an enemy, in which black was black and soldiers was soldiers, and the dead young man had taught them that. I saw pleasure in their grey faces down which the tears ran. I saw that the boy was my old friend Jacob, who had broken into the little mortuary with me, where we had inspected the corpse together. Now he was a member of that fraternity and my tears came and Jessie whispered, 'Little witch, he is too young to know about death, and so are you.' His eyes were swollen and tight shut. He seemed to have been crying under them. His hair was so glossy black in death, because his skin was so pale. He had on his good suit, and there was dust on the lapels. The men who carried him were granite-faced, like justice. Jacob would lie in a cold place, some ice-room, until it was time for the funeral, and time for the funeral men to play out their roles. The funeral which is also a war-dance; the Wake which produces more Sleep. I want to live! but there is only a minute to go now, and it is too late to leave the public house.

I remember the old driver of the ice-lorry. He'd slam the tinny door of the lorry's cab and he'd walk round to take the great tongs off the pile of sacks at the back, and lower the tail-gate. His face was the colour of that sacking, and it was criss-crossed with lines that resembled the weave of the sacking. That so wrinkled a man should have charge of the smooth cool ice! I thought that I was the snow-maiden for the job, I would be the right golden-haired lady in an ice-white shirt to apply the tongs firmly and lift the deep slabs with no more effort than the little old man. I would do this when I had grown up. I knew then that ladies grew to be strong, often. I have seen them since, lifting the bomb-rubble off their men and the children during the bad times. Ice is so clear. In my mind's eye I can see every scale of the great Friday salmon that belonged to the manager of the bank, through the clear ice, on the day that our *butcher's shop was shut. Ice is so short-lived. The man who delivered it looked older than the stars. I wanted to be a lady who delivered the ice. Forty-five seconds to go.*

Forty seconds to go, among the marble pillars in the soldiers' pub of mirrors, vain bastards that they are. Opposite me on a chair is propped Sean's knapsack as though he had just gone outside for a moment and was coming back to me. His name is on it in large letters like the letters on his tombstone. The people are all laughing and drinking and talking about their lives and deciding this and that, distinguishing friend from foe. I am their friend because I love them. I am their foe because I shall kill them. I shall be all things to them, and I shall not myself be exempt. There is a piano playing. My small port and lemon waits patiently in front of me on the marble-topped table with the heavy iron pedestal base, done in fruiting grapes and coiling vines and pouting cherubs who will truly fly through their air; they will be shrapnel. The barmen peep through the little glazed doors fitted above the great mahogany bar: shrapnel. My port and lemon: shrapnel. Indeed the clockwork from the case with the four pillars doubled in my Mother's bedroom mirror has a quiet tick but in thirty seconds' time it will speak decisively from Sean's knapsack and instead of chiming it will detonate the ten sticks of dynamite we took from the little hut in the quarry through the broken wall. Every part of our lives will be slammed into every other part and then there will be a new beginning. The whole butcher's shop will be there, the shambles; the blood will spring like fountains, and there will be flesh sliced thin by flying glass, and joints dismembered, and there will be blossom of flame, and bloody smoke, and eyes will be blown out of heads and skins off backs and babies will be blown out of their mothers' bellies. Blood will flash across the piano-keys that will blow away like black and white leaves. All the little doors will be blown open, the lids and the lips, and the laughing expressions and the calm ones and the sodden ones will all be blown off the faces and the skin will stick on the wall and opposite me is a mirror in which I am watching myself die in twenty seconds from now and watching all the other people die who are watching themselves laughing and spitting and grinding their spit under their heels to show they are not afraid of what lies underneath, and the army will come and the ambulances will come like white ice-houses on wheels and the police will scatter sawdust on the butcher's floor and all the mirrors will be bloody and stumped for an answer and the men standing and the women sitting will be all over the place so they will be collected together in baskets like the Sunday dinner and put on ice and there is a sharp double pain in my back like a serpent's tooth and the sympathy-blood has leapt and fastened its fangs in me and trickles down my childless legs regular as a clock with an almost-silent tick and to answer the blood of those around me who are not yet bleeding and I shall be slammed into the mirror behind me that is gleaming like a great block of ice but how far I shall go into that mirror land I cannot guess but now I know that I was born to suffer what I myself did just like everyone around me and I get to my feet and I shout out to them all 'Stop!' and all their reflections freeze in the mirrors and in one second from now all the hearts in the room will burst.

Chapter two

The water-cure

I

After the evening a year ago when Guy had found Matthew weeping in the pub, had taken him home and watched him drink himself to sleep, they had spent much time together. Guy had called round the next morning and fed his friend coffee; he had found him in a bad state, trembling and sweating, his face ashen. He was talking incoherently about dreams he had had, of criminals and black men, of a cruel fire in a house, and of a blonde woman in blue trousers, who was supernormal in some way, and of the cruel mutilation of two men, and how they had great nails hammered into their bellies, and about the big suit-case of old clothes that had to be put away. 'Dreams have their meaning, Guy; if a man could dream more perhaps he would drink less.'

'Let's both stop drinking, now,' said Guy. He had meditated this for weeks now, seriously worried about his friend. A dream last night had decided him. He was younger and it would cost him less effort than it would Matthew. He refused to examine his feelings about a life without drink, but he wanted his friend to be well. 'We'd be company for each other, then. It'd be good for me.'

'I doubt whether we'd stay acquainted.'

'Oh, it'd have to be a project — like that travel book we were going to write.'

'I'll probably start seeing things

'We'll try and see them together, then. People have been trying to see things, as you put it, from time immemorial. Not everybody has the stomach for drink, you know. Think of all the crystal-gazing, fortune-telling, seance-going, speaking with tongues, medicine-dancing, not to say poetry-writing, that generations and populations have spent their time and their sub-stance in, all the scrying, ritualising, staring at sanded discs, into ink-pools, into the entrails of animals . . .'

'But that's all rubbish . . .'

'Well, so is poetry, if you look at it that way. But it serves a function, and it is a kind of speech beyond speech: nonsense, or nightmare, or revelation. Did the Bible write itself, then? Was it composed by half-amnesic drunkards . . .'

'Maybe it was written by men giving up drink.'

'For these men are not drunk, as you suppose, since it is only the third hour of the day.'

'I love writing poetry,' said Matthew in a subdued voice, 'it doesn't come to me as often as I need it, but when it does come it is like slaking a thirst I never knew I had. It is a wonderful feeling; and alcohol is only the shadow of it. There is a moment when whisky seems to give inspiration, but you know even at that time that there are fumes in your head and lungs which are poison, and that when you drink you are saying goodbye to everything dear and good. It may be that poetry is only the shadow of something else too. Perhaps poetry is the way that I keep that other thing small enough and manageable enough, but still in sight. But I've always hated religion.'

'It's agreed that we shall go into this as agnostics. There's something else, though . . .'

'Well . . .'

'We want to keep our minds on one thing, to concentrate them. I liked what your man said about bees. Since we can't say prayers, we can think of bees. I dreamed last night too. My dream was that there were seven butchers, dressed in white, with blue-and-white aprons, pinned by a pearl button up to their breastbones. They opened a white door that had a big silvery handle like the hold of a ship, and inside it was all furred and frosted, and as the air came out, their breaths fogged it. They marched in and began carrying out big joints of meat, which they arranged on tables whose tops were clean timber that had been scrubbed many times, and which were hacked and notched as with much work of butchers. They carried out the joints of an animal that had been frozen, and with great skill sliced the meat off in chops and joints until the bones and gristle were bare, carrying the meat out to another place where I understood it was bought, cooked and consumed. With great ceremony one of the butchers marched out with the head of the animal. There was no skin on this head, but it had great swept-back horns, and its lidless eyes glared and its lipless teeth smiled. They scooped out the eyes and pared the cheeks, the neck and the scalp of the last remnants, and when the whole skeleton was bare and laid complete in its parts over the block, they stood back in a row, having put down their knives, and looked at me expectantly, from under their seven straw hats. At first I did not know what to do. The cold from the open door was chilling my bones, and my teeth started to chatter. I remembered your doctor and his saying "Think of bees," and my teeth chattering seemed like the hum of a swarm of bees, and my whole body began to tremble. A darkness was gathering round the frame of the white door and on the walls of the white room, and I saw that one of the bearded butchers was bearded with bees. My body grew warmer as the hum grew deeper, and I tasted a sweetness in my mouth. The swarm of bees launched themselves into the air, and swayed like a thick smoke in a cone or small whirlwind. I saw the butcher's beard strip itself off and he was clean-shaven. Then these bees began to line the bare bones on the table, and the bones, clothed with wings, hovered off the wood and settled themselves standing on the floor. The horned head flew to the neck and settled there. I saw the bees hanging in folds beneath the chin like a dewlap. The hum altered in pitch to the lowing of a cow. I thought of udders, that gave honey. I woke. I woke up with that idea, that we should give up drink together, come what may.'

'And that we should think of bees. You've got a start. You've written about them.'

'I've made some poems about bees, yes. The bees helped me, like anything that raises one's spirits so much that the only answer is a poem.'

'Or a drink, or a cigarette, to keep it within reasonable bounds. I think I stopped being a child just about the time I learnt to smoke.' The two men looked at each other with the same innocent look, like the one that made Guy's audience laugh when he said poets were effeminate. Neither of them was aware that to an outsider they seemed not effeminate, but like a kind of enthusiastic and bibulous cherub; not at all grown-up; like children at the parental cocktail-cabinet. Both of them still drank from enthusiasm; neither of them had known what it was like to drink from bone-tiredness or despair, or from lack of anything else to do. It was still for them a naughtiness; though in Matthew the soul had begun to think as pure alcohol would think, that wished nothing but to add to itself for everlasting.

II

You could call it occupational therapy — games to pass the time, while the drink wore off, evaporated from the body, years of it. Guy had dabbled in psychology, of the popular, streamlined variety concerned with 'topdog' versus 'underdog', and thought that Matthew had cast himself as the perfect sly underdog: whose conscience would allow him no pleasure in what he could do well, so he would do it badly, drunk, and get his pleasure while contemplating his diminished accomplishments, which did not look so small from underneath, where underdogs lived. Matthew's topdog, his conscience, was what kept him a kid, and it was this that he was busy replacing with pure alcohol. Guy was the same, but he was younger, and had never been ground down by the process of schoolmastering: which in effect cast the unfortunate teacher as his own topdog, thus simultaneously strengthening the perfectionist in the personality while reducing its credibility. Guy, born at a better time, not having grown up between the wars, or served in a world war, as Matthew had done, had seen less terror and social change. He had never been out of work; he had started earning his living in the affluent sixties, and had the habit of optimism. He got money now by his writing and lecturing; had worked in advertising and journalism. Guy knew he must not become Matthew's topdog; indeed, he respected the older man too much for this to happen. Matthew's conversation was in normal times rich enough to give Guy pause always to consider, and Matthew appreciated this, and had use for Guy's optimism, and never sought to corrupt it. Anyway, now they were not about the perfectionisms of the literary world; they were playing games.

Guy had one particularly strong belief: if this had been shown to be untrue he would have lost that optimism. It was that visions, whether they were visions of the night, dreams, or of the day, hallucinations, were never really arbitrary, but had a meaning. This meaning was usually interpretable, that is, it could be restated in a language that ordinary consciousness was accustomed to, or could become accustomed to in the waking state. Thus, Guy's dream of the butchers could be understood to say that it was time to pare down to the bone, that this stripping down fed the multitudes within, that butchers, those unregarded workers, were operating in sevens, the divine number, and were therefore serving a divine function as sacrificers; and that once the bones were revealed after the carcass had been lifted out of its frozen status (and the ice, he thought, was alcohol), the new life in an unexpected form would clothe the bones and give an alternative nutriment.

But such an interpretation was to him an expedient. It really didn't matter how you interpreted, providing what you said was capacious enough to give the dream-figures their full implications and therefore hold them undiminished in consciousness and memory long enough to adjust that consciousness and its attitudes. If some such 'interpretation' were not given — and, indeed, within its limitations it might very well be correct — then the dream would vanish with all the other vapours of the night. Once it was accepted that the dream had a meaning that extended into the undeveloped portions of one's being, that were sending their messages of fulfilment by this means, and one's conscious mind had accustomed itself to contemplating the dreams and remembering them (if necessary by the mnemonic of psychoanalytic interpretation) then all that was necessary to grow was to dream. The dream experienced, and contemplated like any other experience, like a love-affair or a cinema film, would work its magic. This magic might come by a realisation, for instance, that the shrill voice of conscience screaming at one for academic perfection was not only one's mother's, but one's grandfather howling his unsatisfied wants through her down the generations, if that was one's condition; or it might come by a spurt of laughter at the comical images of a dream that suddenly, with an energy, released one from an attitude, an expression, a silly hat, an odd and damaging habit, an old pair of slippers that justly irritated one's spouse; or it might come by a nudge of warning at the edge of intuition: a quick replay of a situation that was becoming dangerous and which, one realised, one had passed through before, unknowingly, many times. Dreaming was a way of thinking in pictures, with feeling, sensuously. A dream could simply mean that one woke up feeling better than one had for days, and the value of that was not only in itself, but that the practised dreamer would know that an inward adjustment had been made; it was not simply that the sun was shining brightly outside.

A subsection of Guy's credo was that mental disturbances, and physical ones too, could often be caused by a *compression of the dream,* as though a tape were being played very fast, and the beautiful melody it contained was distorted to a scream, or a cinema film of the world's masterpieces of painting were run so fast that they were in effect all played simultaneously, and produced a total blackness, like a depression. It was therefore necessary to slow down the messages, to allow them to emerge at an intelligible speed. This was why Matthew's DTs so leapt out at him. And this is how Guy and Matthew between them justified entering their new playground.

Guy drew up a list of methods that would allow the dream or visionary faculties to stretch their muscles, to feel their freedom. The two friends would observe and record this process; it would occupy them while they were growing out of drink, but not only that, it would make the process of growth itself visible to them. They would be careful not to intervene; they were merely obeying the command 'know thyself'. The list of techniques included, of course, poetry, the contemplation of the language precipitated by the freer energies of the psyche, but this magic mirror they had stared into for most of their adult lives, and it was both too familiar and too precious to become part of their game. Poetry, they suspected, was an image of a place or condition they wished one day to arrive at, in full self-possession. It was more like an end than a means.

Meditation went on their list, though one of its varieties

was prayer (and therefore presumably as precious to others as poetry was to them). The nature of prayer was for God alone, and not, like poetry, visible to a reader; and they were agnostics. Dreaming itself was a skill to be cultivated, and Guy had already used methods he found effective. Then there was the crystal ball; one could buy very good crystal balls at the Occult Shop, big, inexpensive, plastic ones. That was the place to buy either a planchette or a ouija board too; dowsing pendulums and rods; and what about some books on sex-magic? It was all fun. It was almost intoxicating. It would give something for idle thoughts, and idle fingers groping for a drink, to do.

Matthew said, 'There's one way that we can make all these oddities our own. Dozens of people have done fruitless work with these expedients. I have a way to test an idea like that. It's to see whether Groucho is friendly to it. Can you see him? Say "Think of bees, Groucho." Now look, he's leaning forward in that crouch, with his black frock-coat, his black greasepaint eyebrows and moustache, his black cigar firmly in his mouth. Say "Think of bees, Groucho." The eyebrows waggle, the cigar pulls out slowly in a descending arc, and now you can hear Dr Hackenbush saying with a deep considering nasal twang, "I want you to think of bees, friend, and that will be twenty dollars." Can you hear him saying it now?'

'Yes,' said Guy.

'That's good enough for me, then,' said Matthew.

III

The Occult Shop looked as though it had a hard time surviving. Guy and Matthew were not quite sober when they arrived; after all, they had not started not drinking yet, could not, until they had purchased their equipment. Matthew lingered by the shop window sniggering at some of the titles displayed. 'Would you buy books of poetry with titles like these?' he asked.

'Think of it as you would one of the storerooms of the British Museum,' said Guy. 'Poetry is one of the things you can't translate.' He pointed at a small blue fibreglass figure of an Egyptian mummy, carved with signs and with a half-smile on its face. The forearms were crossed on the breast, and held implements, which looked like small agricultural flails. A card propped under the figure said: 'Purchase your Ushabti figure here.' And in small letters: 'This is your dream friend. Contemplate this ancient figure, a replica of a tomb-ornament of the XVIIIth Dynasty of Ancient Egypt, and he will come to life in your dreams and assist you in the other world. Full instructions included. "Verily I am here and will come whithersoever thou biddest me."' Matthew had his nose up against the pane to read the card like a small boy outside a toyshop, and his spectacles gleamed.

'I want one of those,' he said; 'it can stand on the bedside table instead of that intolerable green bug.'

Inside, the shop was stuffed with books, many of them having nothing to do with the occult. It was as though a much smaller occult store was struggling with a large ordinary second-hand bookshop. Romantic novelettes of the thirties and forties were growing down from the ceiling, and travel-books were marching out of the corners. However, to a little higher than eye-level, the shelves were stuffed solid with the kind of titles that Matthew had complained of. ('Imagine a crude translation of the Bible,' muttered Guy.) Megalithic stones were in: *The Living Stones of Land's End* ('by Dr Stanley, I presume,' snickered Matthew); *The Walking Monuments of Olden Time* ('Nelson went for a stroll, you see, and left his column empty, so somebody tried to steal it, was seen, and chased up the Mall, dropping cylindrical bits. That is the origin of they Lunnun stones, boy.'). Earth-currents, flying saucers, and Bermuda triangles were rife: *Magnetic Monsters of the Midwest; The Flying Saucer Spinoff* ('Saucers are not my cup of tea,' said Guy; 'They do cheer the inebriated, though,' replied Matthew); *Chasms in the Crust*. And there were a great many instructions related to the friends' own project, bound in lurid covers: *Personal Witchcraft: I can make You a Sorcerer; Shuddering: A New Method of Astral Communion*. Matthew picked up a copy of the last, shuddered, and put it down again.

'It's mad, isn't it?' he whispered to Guy. The lady behind the counter was looking at them. They suspected her of believing them to be not quite sober, which was absolutely true; so now they moved with great care, and replaced books with exaggerated courtesy. 'Remember, remember,' said Guy; 'look, here's a crystal.' He took down a small, slightly scratched and yellowed transparent globe, and took it up to the counter. The lady, who wore a long, grubby black skirt, a black T-shirt pleasantly full of breast, and a colourful embroidered waistcoat, smiled at him quite without magical guile. She said that this 'crystal' was only a sample, which had been on show for some time. The light had yellowed it, but the new ones that had been kept in their boxes were quite bright and shining, and she showed him. He told her that they wanted to buy some other things as well, including a Ushabti figure, and went back to Matthew. He looked rather like the Ushabti himself, because he had a little half-smile on his face, and gripped in his hands were two bent copper wires that were gyrating madly, sleeved in their slippery polythene handles. 'Look!' he said, 'it's dowsing. You wander about over drainpipes trying to hold these steady, and your muscles pick up the water-feelings in the ground, and the wires swing. I can't keep them still! I must have the shakes. I'd like to try them; the blurb is quite sensible, for once. Written by an engineer.' In the end they took the crystal and the box of dowsing-rods, a book on automatic writing (with the unfortunate title *Scribes of the Unknown,* which Matthew said was a message direct to them, since he liked helping unknown writers, and was not even too well known himself), another one on 'sex-magic' *(The Temple of the Bed);* and after they had asked to be shown the ouija board and the planchette, decided on the latter. The ouija was merely a stiff board about the size of a coffee-table, and printed with the letters of the alphabet, arranged in a crescent-shape along one edge. There were also some quite gratuitous designs showing aichemical retorts and a skull resting on an open, leather-bound volume, and it was these as much as anything that caused them to reject this instrument. Matthew simply closed his eyes and turned away. The board was coated with plastic, and one was supposed to let an upturned tumbler slide about it, telling out the letters, steered by the sitters' fingertips.

The planchette was much neater. A small wooden shape like a heart or artist's palette in polished wood was fitted with two castor-bearings. In it was drilled a hole fitted with a tightening-screw, and the lady explained that you slid in here a carpenter's soft pencil. The sitters then placed their fingers lightly on the board, and, if they were in the right frame of mind (a passive alertness), the fingertips would (as with the ouija tumbler) swing the palette about on a sheet of paper placed beneath it. And it would leave marks which might become designs and drawings, or even writing, she said. Whether this writing came from spirits or from the sitters' unconscious minds was a moot point: claims were made for both, and if the results were interesting, who cared? She herself had tried it, and had contacted an entity claiming to be Shelley's ghost, who gave her advice about writing poetry. This was useless to her as, far from being interested in verse, she had the disability, she said sadly, of being hardly able to fit one sentence to another when it came to writing letters or suchlike, though she was a great talker, she said, and liked reading. She had read most of the serious books in the shop, but was just no good with a pencil. 'Then who was this Shelley?' She didn't know, she said, but whoever it was it seemed to be a man, and quite good at writing things down for her through the planchette, some of which she noticed came from books that she had just read. Oh, she got bored with this, and gave it up; though she had got quite fond of Shelley, and liked to think of him as a customer who had come into the shop, and whom she had enjoyed talking to, but might never see again. Matthew remarked that the unconsciousness of sensible people behaved sensibly.

He had his finger in an old book, and showed the spine to Guy: it was on Ancient Egypt, and was by an author called Massey. Inside, at the place Matthew marked, Guy read:

'Mythical representation did not begin with "stories of human adventure", as Mr Spencer puts it, nor with human figures at all, but with the phenomena of external nature, that were represented by means of animals, birds, reptiles and insects, which had demonstrated the possession of superhuman faculties and powers. The origin of various superstitions and customs seemingly insane can be traced to sign-language. In many parts of England it is thought necessary to "tell the Bees" when a death has occurred in the house, and to put the hives into mourning. The present writer has known the housewife to sally forth into the garden with warming-pan and key and strips of crêpe to "tell the Bees", lest they should take flight, when one of the inmates of the house had died. We must seek an explanation for this in the symbolism of Egypt that was carried forth orally to the ends of the earth. The Bee was anciently a zootype of the Soul which was represented as issuing forth from the body in that form or under that type. There is a tradition that the Bees alone of all animals descended from Paradise. In the Engadine, Switzerland, it is said that the Souls of men go forth from this world and return to it in the form of Bees. Virgil, in the Fourth Book of the Georgics, celebrates the Bee that never dies, but ascends alive into heaven. That is the typical Bee which was an image of the Soul. It was the Soul, as Bee, that alone ascended into heaven or descended from thence. The Bee is certainly one form of the Egyptian Abait, or Bird-Fly, which is a guide and pilot to the Souls of the Dead on their way to the fields of Aarru. It was a figure of Lower Egypt as the land of honey, thence a fitting guide to the celestial fields of the Aarru-Paradise. It looks as if the name for the Soul, Ba, in Egyptian, may be identical with our word Bee. Ba is honey determined by the Bee-sign, and Ba is also the Soul. The Egyptians made use of honey as a means of embalming the dead. Thus the Bee, as a zootype of the Soul, became a messenger of the dead and a mode of communication with the ancestral Spirits. Talking to the Bees in this language was like speaking with the Spirits of the dead, and, as it were, commending the departed one to the guidance of the Bees, who as honey-gatherers naturally knew the way to the Elysian fields and the meads of Amaranth that flowed with milk and honey . . . Thus the *inventor* of honey in this world led the way to the fields of flowers in the next.'

'Bird-fly. That's good poetry. How much is this book?' asked Matthew, holding out the dusty and crumbling volume.

'It's fifty pounds, I'm afraid,' said the lady.

'Pity,' said Matthew: 'I opened it just at the right page. My finger was thinking of bees. How very like a pupa that Ushabti mummy is wrapped. Do the Egyptian souls not have wings when they are unwrapped? Isis has wings, and the deceased is, when he is risen, said to be Osirified. I'm sure I've seen the Ka shown with wings. But would they be Bee-wings? "Bird-fly". Very nice indeed. The best of both worlds. Oh, it should be called Ushabti Street,' sang Matthew, happily, as the two friends emerged into the dusty sunlight of Shipton Street, near the British Museum, clutching to themselves their archaic paraphernalia.

IV

The dowsing equipment was highly amusing. Water-divining seemed like golf, an open-air sport in which middle-aged men could get mild exercise without exhausting themselves, and absorb the scenery as well. Guy and Matthew started their practice as the enclosed booklet instructed them. They were to find a place with known water-courses running beneath. One's garden, if one knew the way the drains went, or the road outside, where there were all sorts of manholes and guttering, were useful elementary sites. One gripped the bent wires, which were sheathed into plastic handles in such a way that they swung in a horizontal plane. First of all, one must practise walking with these wires pointing parallel to the way one was walking, rather like tram-lines between which one strode. At first this was not easy; the pivoting of the wires was sensitive, and they waved about wildly if the wrists were not held still; nor must they be quite rigid, otherwise unevennesses in the terrain would make the wires swing. Guy found himself sufficiently steady; Matthew felt, as he had in the shop, that his 'shakes' from drinking and tobacco might disqualify him. On the morning they tried the rods first, he was indeed rather tremulous, but Guy saw that the shakes eased as he became interested.

After learning to walk evenly with the rods, one had to learn a much more difficult skill: detachment. The book recommended that the practitioner should contemplate the wrists and the rods held in front of him; should not intervene; should not regard them as merely his wrists and rods, or be too pleased that he was dowsing, or believe that he was doing anything else but watching sensitive pointers, as one might watch dials in an aeroplane or a train-cab. Then, said the book, the instruments would indicate of their own accord when one passed over water. Ideally, one of a pair of companions should know the verifiable water-courses underground, and the other not; there was then a check. But in the absence of such controls, honesty to oneself was the only guard. Results without checks were bound not to be so impressive, as one could always put down any reactions experienced to 'autosuggestion'. Nevertheless the movements were involuntary, and in due course, it was averred, the man who was going to be a dowser would contemplate movements that sprang from his deepest levels unmoved by thoughts of personal gratification, but with a true scientific curiosity, and, it was hinted, if he were truly responsive to the electromagnetic fields that might or might not exist round flowing water, a person might experience a particular 'dowsing' feeling that could not be obtained in any other manner. Even this must not overcome the mind of the dowser, who must remain calm in his endeavour to magnify responses that were natural to us all, by his attention and by the sensitive instrumentation of the dowsing-rods. Indeed, in some people reaction was so strong that, not having an explanation for it, they dismissed such feelings as 'atmosphere', a 'bad' place or a 'good' one, and shrugged the matter off. Frequently these feelings — sometimes manifesting as ghosts or other apparitions, kobalds, fairies, nature spirits — could be explained as the forces produced by underground rivers and caves, or deposits of metallic ore, which a dowser would detect by his rod, and were monstrified into terrifying images by cowardly or unpractised people. This, to Guy, was like 'compression of the dream' to which he attributed many disturbances that were commonly classified as psychiatric; he thought that in using the rods he would turn a corner, so to speak, and realise that many of the feelings he commonly had as apprehensions or little visitations of joy that were mysterious, would be found to be actual perceptions of objects or influences in the environment: just as a weather-sensitive person's feelings are registering air-pressure like any barometer, with its column of mercury, or vacuum-drum and pointer. Matthew was particularly interested in the sections in the booklet which mentioned how sensitive many animals were to underground water, and how bees would follow the passage of a subterranean stream up to the source, and drink there.

Millie and Guy had a garden with a lawn, and this was the obvious place for their first practice. Guy knew roughly where the drainage from the house ran, but as an added source of manifestation he buried the garden hose-pipe along one of the long narrow flowerborders that ran down to the garden's bottom, where there was a small stream.

It was a sunny, cool morning. Matthew had had no drink the night before, nor had Guy: their first drinkless day. Millie and he had heard Matthew shouting during the night, and she had tiptoed into the spare room to see how he was — they all thought it better that he should stay with them for the time being.

'We should try and find him a girl to look after him,' said Millie at breakfast.

'That would be fair on neither of them,' was Guy's rejoinder.

She took him up a cup of strong coffee, and it was not long before Matthew came stumbling down. He had shaved carefully, and his face was tight and glossy from the aftershave, but the colour of the skin was ashen. Millie put scrambled eggs in front of him. He closed his eyes for a moment as if dazzled by the yellow colour; opened them again, said, 'That would be very nice. Thank you,' and began to eat with some appetite. Millie told Guy afterwards that it was no wonder Matthew was hungry — he must have been working hard all night in his dreams: the bed was wet as though he had run a mile in the bedclothes, and the pillow was as sopping and almost as smelly as if he had urinated on it.

Matthew looked out of the window at the sunny lawn. He reached into his jacket pocket and took out his bottle of capsules, shook them to hear them rattle, pretended that the bottle was a timepiece which he affected to consult, holding it to his ear, winding its neck, finally unscrewing it and taking one of the drug doses, sealed in dark gelatine. 'Dowsabell, Dowsabell, rise up in the morn, / Come out to the Dowsing and get your skirt torn,' he said with an upward flash of his eyes through lowered spectacles, as though it might not be funny to them, but he took liberty to find, without discourtesy, the situation amusing.

Millie relaxed in a deckchair while the two men struggled with the vibrant and wildly-swinging rods. Matthew simply could not master them — the ends of the bent wires, because of the way he held his wrists, crossed immediately and got tangled up. Guy remarked that he was getting the dowsing reaction without stirring a step. Matthew thought that was because he was already on the water-wagon, or was it because drying-out got your wires crossed? Guy suggested that Matthew might sit down instead and keep quiet while he, Guy, had a go. The taller man held the wires steady without difficulty and, walking slowly and with great care, paced across the lawn. He knew where the manhole was where the drains left the house, and he knew the outlet by the fence to the bottom right of the garden, and he tried not to visualise where (if the pipes were straight) the drain ran under the lawn. He paced across once, turned and then came back again, the rods rigid and unmoved as train-tracks. 'You're walking like a man marching between sentry-boxes,' called out Millie. Matthew was watching intently, which pleased Guy. He adopted a slouching manner, and immediately the wires crossed: he recovered their position and thought to himself: 'I stroll along the promenade with an independent air, / And all the girls declare / He must be a millionaire,' which he felt approximated to the right attitude. As he passed by the kitchen window, to his amazement the wires crossed, and in two paces uncrossed again. Unbelieving, he walked slowly backwards over the same spot, and they crossed again. The others had not seen this, as his back was to them in this position. He laid the wires carefully down on the grass to mark the spot, and Millie came up to him. 'It works, doesn't it? Can I try?' She took the rods and found it easy, too, to hold them parallel. Then slowly she walked across the place where Guy had registered water. As if keeping pace with her movement, the rods crossed gradually as she passed over the spot, separated, and crossed again as she returned. Matthew was there by now. There were spots of colour in his cheeks, and his eyes were alive and quite Groucho-like behind his glasses. 'That's a good way of detecting an empty pipe,' he remarked; 'you can't be dowsing water because nobody's using the drain.' 'Yes we can,' said Millie, 'the bathroom tap drips.'

Guy peeled a twig and set it up at the bottom of the garden

where the concrete drain outlet was. Standing on the manhole outside the kitchen, you could see that their marked spot was, in fact, exactly where the drain would run. Millie now took the rods and, closing her eyes firmly, began to walk to and fro over the grass, in a meander curve. Guy kept pace with her, and had taken out of his pocket little slivers of white plastic, which he was sticking in the ground at the point where Millie's rods crossed, and where they uncrossed. In a while she had reached the bottom of the garden, and Guy told her to open her eyes, otherwise she'd walk straight into the stream.

Back up the lawn stretched a perfectly straight double line of little white plastic markers, showing the drain's path under the soil from manhole to garden outlet.

'What about that!' shouted out Guy to his friend, who was smoking among the deckchairs. Matthew started up, as if he had been sleeping or dozing, with the kind of little shout that a disturbed sleeper might give. 'What! Oh, beautiful. I wish I could do some. But I'm trembling a bit, I'm afraid. Look.' He held out his stained fingers with the cigarette between them, and the shiver of his hand made the smoke rise and lie over itself in flattened layers, the shudder recorded on the air.

'Matthew . . .' said Guy, and went to the little hazel-tree near the water. He took out a penknife and cut off a forked twig, which he cleaned of its leaves. 'Matthew . . . hold this and walk over the ground. Hold it like the old dowser in the photo. Just relax and see what happens. You can see that it really works.'

Matthew took the fork, and held the two ends of it gently in his hands with the stubby end pointing forwards, as Guy showed him. He began walking over the line of markers, his hands and arms trembling still.

'Millie,' said Guy, whispering, 'pop inside and turn some taps on, so that there's a lot of water going down the drain. See if that makes a difference.' She went in, and Matthew crossed the line of markers again, and as he did so his arm jumped a little, and he looked surprised. Again he crossed the markers, and this time the rod rose steeply in his hands, as though it were a model aeroplane he was flying by gripping its wings. The twig soared upwards, and Matthew looked delighted.

53

'Christ, boy,' he said, 'this is bloody funny.' Again and again he crossed the line; his eyebrows were plainly visible in his surprise above the curved upper rims of his glasses, and again and again the rod stood up. Guy went over and, as the older man crossed again, tried to hold the twig still by taking hold of the end. The impulse in Matthew's hands was so strong that the stick snapped. 'Christ, boy,' he said again, 'you've spoilt the only good erection I've had for ten years.'

Millie came out and asked, 'How did it go?'

'Marvellous,' said Guy, turning to her; 'he must be a natural dowser — look at the broken twig.' Matthew had gone down the garden with Guy's penknife to cut another. 'The volume of water when you turned the tap on must have broken through all his resistance.'

'Well, that's remarkable,' said Millie, looking very psychological; 'there were no extra taps on then.'

'Why?' asked Guy, surprised.

'A wasp or bee or something had got into the sink and was drinking the splashes, and I had to get rid of it out of the window. I came to tell you that I've only just turned the water on.'

Matthew had stopped walking the old route with his new dowser's twig. He had stopped at the flowerbed where Guy had earlier buried his hose-pipe.

'Just a minute,' said Guy, laying a hand on Millie's shoulder; 'tell me what happens when I turn on the garden tap.' He disappeared behind the tool-shed. Suddenly Matthew gave one of his nightmare cries and fell backwards as if shot. Millie hurried towards him where he lay on the grass. He'd clearly fainted. Guy came out from behind the shed and started runfling towards them. Inside the house he could hear the doorbell ringing. Matthew was unconscious, but far from mute. He was shouting with confused cries they could make nothing of. Suddenly he opened his eyes wide. His glasses had fallen off, leaving his face looking strangely nude.

'Meave!' he said, 'Meave? Guy? Millie. It's you. Oh, that was awful. I thought I'd never wake up. It was as though a bomb had gone off in my head, and my head was made of painted glass. The pieces came flying and buzzing through the air and cut the world to pieces.'

There was a loud cough behind them. A girl with cropped, honey-coloured hair and dressed in faded T-shirt and jeans had come into the garden from the back door behind the tool-shed. 'I'm Meave,' she said. 'I was to meet Matthew here. I'm from the hospital.' They saw she had bare feet. 'I'm a friend of the doctor he saw. Let me help.'

'I'm all right,' said Matthew, getting up with dignity. 'Let's go inside and have a nice glass of water.'

Chapter three

Sorcerer's apprentices

I

It turned out that there was to be little contact between the two friends from that time in the garden when the dowsing began everything and Meave and Matthew went off together, up to that evening a year later when Guy, exhausted by trance communication, and Millie, full of intellectual reserve, were shown the completion of their automatic script by an agitated and pale Matthew in flight from the Institute. There was no question of a put-up job between the two men to convince Millie. She had to admit that. The two scripts fitted so exactly together and had been written miles apart. The awful imminence of the diminishing seconds to the bomb blast, the tone, the locale, the quiet madness, all fitted. Why were the men so upset by the communication, when it gave them such a perfect example of 'cross correspondence': of a coherent communication received in separate portions by people who were not in contact? For Guy, it was that he was new to the slipping in and out of trance; it was still a blind submission to the unknown for him, and his body rebelled, and had not learnt to conserve its resources in a state, as it were, of sleeping upright. Nor did he relish the free floating madness of this spirit, whether it was in truth a discarnate entity, a telepathic communication, or simply a tiny stratum of madness in himself, dislodged by his recent practices and fermenting like yeast: that was his fear. With Matthew it was simply: he thought he recognised the bomber.

Matthew had left with Meave that afternoon of the dowsing. Later that week there was a phone call that he was moving in with her 'and the twins' at the Institute. Guy asked whether he was drinking and Matthew said firmly, 'No need, no need.' When he was asked if he was playing the occult games and whether they were helpful he said quite crossly, 'They're not games, Guy.' Guy was worried, and wondered whether either he or Matthew was being had, but decided that he had no cause to complain, whatever happened now: he had done his best. Had he done his best for himself, though? He had planchette, crystal ball, sex-magic manual, dowsing rods, and no friend to play with. Millie adopted her scientific manner and remarked that she would be delighted to investigate with him, providing she was not required to believe anything specific in advance. When Guy asked her about sex-magic, she first of all wondered exactly what that might be, then said that she expected no diminution in her sexual relationship with Guy, but would maintain the same agnostic stance, if he didn't mind. He was welcome to try almost anything.

Matthew's attack during the dowsing had been like an epilepsy. When they discussed the experience afterwards, he said that it was like a hammer blow to the head and like an explosion within in answer to the blow. He said that it came all at once, and there were many other components which only unpacked themselves in the hours afterwards. He remembered, for instance, that just before the fit he had been bending over the soil of the flower bed, and had noticed for the first time what rainbow colours the individual grains of soil reflected in the sunlight, and how rich, complex and deep were the tones the rainbows made up when they were fastened together as humus, melding everything to a brown colour that seemed to speak the word 'fertility'. Then came the flash. Guy had told him that this coincided with the turning on of the hose tap, but Matthew simply nodded and said, 'Oh yes.' When he woke up, he said, he had felt that he had burst out of the fringes of a crowd of people all speaking at once, the impression of which was exactly like the soil: each member of the crowd had spoken in clear sparkling tones, but all together it had simply made a fertile noise, a deep and loud hum, like an infinite hive. Guy told him about the confused cries that had burst from him while he was on the ground: Matthew remarked that, well, he must have been shouting with the best of them. He looked thoughtful and said that more people ought to listen instead of talking all the time, and he repeated the word 'listen' slowly a couple of times, like a child trying syllables that he had never used before. He was like someone who had been concussed. He said too that with the voices were many faces, and when he broke out of the crowd it was because he had been following one face that drew him, and that was Meave's. Looking at her he said, 'I was more surprised than I have ever been to see you standing there. I thought the face I was chasing in my dream would fade away, instead it became solid.' 'You knew I was coming,' said Meave. Guy asked whether Matthew had been thinking of bees again. As soon as Guy had caught sight of Meave he began to think of her as the bee lady: the nap of her cropped head gave exactly the impression of the velvet hair on the back and shoulders of the honey bee, and her head was rounded and rather small, which added to the impression. He felt it was an opinion he could not share with Matthew; it was, he realised, the first observation of its kind that he had felt he had to keep back from his friend. When they were together recognitions and images flowed between them, most of them scurrilous, a lot of them about women; this time Guy wanted to keep his peace, though he was filled to bursting when Meave remarked that she had to get back to her brood before teatime ('And is there honey still for tea?' would have been his cue to Matthew, and both would have recognised immediately how her appearance was involved in the quotation, and everything else about her, for everlasting). Then Meave put on a black openwork shawl that gave exactly the impression of black veined bees' wings, and Guy almost spoke.

When Meave and Matthew had gone, Guy went out on to the lawn to pull out the plastic markers. He picked up the rods to try again, but could not settle his mind. Matthew had left his hazel fork on the grass, and Guy picked this up and brought it inside as well. He felt as though his friend had been snatched away out of his ken, and this is how it proved in the subsequent, doubtful months, before Matthew's precipitate return with his automatic writing.

Guy knew that he and Matthew were going to develop in parallel. They were too close for it to be otherwise. He made some enquiries about Meave, and about David, the elderly doctor who had recommended bee-thinking. David ran a kind of informal clinic or school, known as the Institute, in an old house at the edge of the town. Rumour had it that people did what they liked there, and the only thing that rumour found good to say about the establishment was that neither drink nor drugs were allowed. There were open meetings held for meditation; there were seances and lectures; and there were therapy groups over which David presided without, so they said, ever saying a word. David had special pupils. One of these was Meave, who was studying with him to be an analyst; and her brother, Simon, was another. Two adolescent twins lived there also, but what relationship they had to the others was not clear. Guy felt jealous that Matthew had been whisked off towards these opportunities by such knowledgeable people. But he was sure he could work adequately on his own. In bed that night, it pleased him to think of the way the rods he held had swung together, it seemed, of their own accord. As he sank into sleep, Guy realised that they were not the instrument, but that he was, so deep in his body that only sleep could reveal anything of the way he, and all others, were plunged into the water circuits of the sky and the ground. And this was his dream, of human people walking over the earth, dressed in great clothes of water magnetism, with high rainbow collars that touched the clouds, and long sleeves that trailed the ground, and spread over it, swept through it and below it, each garment being a part of the great river that flowed both down below and on high, through the firmament above the earth, and beneath it.

II

Guy still had the dowsing equipment, the crystal ball, the manuals on sex-magic and automatic writing, the planchette, the Ushabti figure. He didn't think Matthew would want any of them. No doubt they had their own apparatus at David's Institute or whatever it was. Guy would work on his own, and work, also, not to drink. Millie was all for this, providing, she said, that he didn't become too calm.

Before he did any more of this work, Guy wanted to settle in his mind what his target was. The problem he had set himself was to know more; and he believed that this would have to do with knowing more about the place poetry came from, though poetry itself was not his aim. Matthew's interiors had set their own problem; Matthew unknown had asked Matthew known unkindly, 'What about these gross green insects, then?' Without a doubt other questions had been posed in the past by Matthew's subterraneans, questions to which Matthew had given the frequent evasive reply 'Have another whisky!' and perhaps because drunkenness was a reasonable facsimile at times of inspiration, the subterraneans had not immediately refused. Recently they had, however — hence the insects and other problems — and had indicated very clearly that they would prefer nothing further to drink, thank you. Then Matthew, rather than consulting the bottle, had agreed to ask Water a question, and the reply he had got had come all at once, and thrown him to the ground, and sent him off to the Institute, and, Guy (with that little touch of envy) supposed, changed his life. He would find out more about this later.

Guy was not provided with such a decisive confrontation, such an extreme problem which, if stood up to in the right manner, might turn into a door that would open on another life. But what did most deeply trouble him in his life? Was there anything that seemed archaic and undeveloped, full of energy that was not understood, and must be ridden to be known, like a wild horse? Was there some deep, unresolved irrationality that could be his doorway? Matthew had been possessed by the insects, in effect — Guy had a sudden vision of his friend in a hospital bed, tied down, his eyes vacant, and instead of speech coming from his mouth, a dry rustling, like the busy chafing of legs and wing-cases. And then Matthew had been possessed by Water. Was Guy not to be possessed by something, that he did not possess? In a sense he was, by almost everything worthwhile. Where did poetry come from? Where sex? There was his enthusiastic skin, that led him sometimes into erotic eccentricities, since it was a very powerful sexual feeling he got when he walked in the warm summer rain, and let his clothes grow wet, and clasp him, as though the sky were wrapping him round. Once, when he was a boy, and coming back from cricket at school, along a little woodland path, he had heard a stream tinkling in the bushes, and he had gone into the black bushes out of the cricketing sunlight, and seen there a clear small stream running by the side of a little jet black mudbank, and in his white clothes he had mysteriously allowed himself to slide into that mud, he couldn't tell why, and as he became black and of the earth, and the caress of earth and water slipped over his daytime appearance masking it with a firm touch, he had felt an exquisite sensation in his loins that was totally indescribable, like a delicious taste that was a solid object with a certain roughness to it. It was the feeling he had had in 'wet dreams'. He had no recollection of what his mother said when he got home; he must have been punished, but could remember nothing of it. Later on, as a man, this feeling sometimes came about during sex, among all the other feelings, and sometimes he could cause it to come with the fantasy that he and his partner, dressed in white, were sinking into river mudbanks. But it was never after that first experience so strong, and there were other urgent and more complex sensations that overlaid it. On the one occasion when he had drunkenly persuaded a sexual partner to make love in the mud with him, it was almost but not quite disaster. She repented her party clothes at the last moment, when it was already too late, and they were actually beginning to sink; she panicked, they both did, when they seemed out of their depth. They had sprawled to land, and there was a moment when she had smeared her hands upwards over her breasts and her silvery blouse when he felt that paradoxical sweetness deep inside him, but she looked terrifyingly cross. Then she laughed at the way he looked, all shaggy and heavy with the river stuff, like a cross between the Frankenstein Monster and Poseidon, so it turned out all right as a jape, and they both crept home, he taking out gritty keys at the front door. They got under the shower together, stripping their stained clothes off under the warm water, and thoroughly enjoyed themselves after all. But it had not become part of his sexual repertory, thank goodness, though for a little time, when he was depressed and between affairs, before he settled down with Millie, it did become a little bit of an obsession, and he thought his ideal partner would be found in the water and the mud. He had written a poem about this, which had seemed important to him at the time.

THE IDEA OF ENTROPY AT MAENPORTH BEACH

'C'est elle! Noire et pourtant lumineuse'
A boggy wood as full of springs as trees.
Slowly she slipped into the muck.
It was a white dress, she said, and that was not right.
Leathery polished mud, that stank as it split.
It is a smooth white body, she said, and that is not right,
Not quite right; I'll have a smoother,
Slicker body, and my golden hair
Will sprinkle rich goodness everywhere.
So slowly she backed into the mud.

If it were a white dress, she said, with some little black,
Dressed with a little flaw, a smut, some swart
Twinge of ancestry, or if it were all black
Since I am white, but — it's my mistake.
So slowly she slunk, all pleated, into the muck.

The mud spatters with rich seed and ranging pollens.
Black darts up the pleats, black pleats
Lance along the white ones, and she stops
Swaying, cut in half. Is it right, she sobs
As the fat, juicy, incredibly tart muck rises
Round her throat and dims the diamond there?
It is right, so she stretches her white neck back
And takes a deep breath once and a one step back.
Some golden strands afloat pull after her.

The mud recoils, lies heavy, queasy, swart.
But then this soft blubber stirs, and quickly she comes up
Dressed like a mound of lickerish earth,
Swiftly ascending in a streaming pat
That grows tall, smooths brimming hips, and steps out
On flowing pillars, darkly draped.
And then the blackness breaks open with blue eyes
Of this black Venus rising helmeted in night

Who as she glides grins brilliantly, and drops
Swatches superb as molasses on her path.

Who is that negress running on the beach
Laughing excitedly with teeth as white
As the white waves kneeling, dazzled, to the sands?
Clapping excitedly the black rooks rise,
Running delightedly in slapping rags
She sprinkles substance, and the small life flies!

She laughs aloud, and bares her teeth again, and cries:
Now that I am all black, and running in my richness
And knowing it a little, I have learnt
It is quite wrong to be all white always;
And knowing it a little, I shall take great care
To keep a little black about me somewhere.
A snotty nostril, a mourning nail will do.
Mud is a good dress, but not the best.
Ah, watch, she runs into the sea. She walks
In streaky white on dazzling sands that stretch
Like the whole world's pursy mud quite purged.
The black rooks coo like doves, new suns beam
From every droplet of the shattering waves,
From every crystal of the shattered rock.
Drenched in the mud, pure white rejoiced,
From this collision were new colours born,
And in their slithering passage to the sea
The shrugged-up riches of deep darkness sang.

Finding a lady in the water and the earth: that was the image. It
could be that it was telling him, in a rather more comely form
than Matthew's insects, that dowsing was one of his explorer's
paths. After all, one dowsed with one's whole body; it was the
natural reaction of one's tissues to the presence of water in
the earth. This natural tug or impulse had been exiled by the
conscious mind, but would make its presence felt by feelings,
feeling tones or poetic images, sexual obliquities as if one had
come within reach of the aura of one's love, her atmosphere.

It might be regressive — 'stick in the mud' — but it was also seeking an earth-mother beyond persons, to leap back from her womb into the world again with gladness — or so his reverie ran. Matthew's experience, then, was a kind of birth trauma — a concussion. Guy flicked open the sex-magic manual and ran his eye over the index. 'Dowsing' was there, to his surprise. On the indicated page 'Think Magically,' it exhorted him, 'think always in reversals. In any enjoyment think of sorrow; if your clothes are white and clean, think of them saturated with mud; if you are sober, think drunk; if you are dry, become a dowser.' Evidently other people have had these feelings, thought Guy; I must go through with it. He realised with pleasure that he had been thinking the matter through like an open-minded sceptic; like Millie, even; and he realised that in much of his interior dialogue, the other voice was hers.

III

Millie was out at her afternoon job at the college library. She would not be home much before eight, as she liked to take a meal at the canteen there, and read a little. His meal was in the oven for when he wanted it. He turned the taps in the kitchen on full, took the rods down from the shelf and went out into the garden. He thought he would begin by detecting the water, as before, though now he realised his aim was a vision of water, more than a sensitivity to it. He wanted the eyes of his flesh to open to water sight, if that were possible. It was not to be done in a spirit of curiosity, he saw, as his enthusiasm mounted, but of communion. That was what was so revolting about the various treatises on sale at the Occult Shop: they were cockily knowing, the whole pack of them. What impiety! Communion and understanding with something larger than oneself was the aim, he thought, looking up at the sky: I stand under the sources of all the rivers; as a large fleece of cloud, gold-tinged, swept over his head.

He filled his shirt-pocket with the little plastic markers, and fastened the hose-pipe to its tap, unreeling the rubber snake down the length of the garden, and adjusting its nozzle to 'flow' rather than 'spray'. It reached to a flattening of the lawn, just above the banks of the little stream. He went back and turned the tap on full, watching the nozzle in the coiled end thrash about. 'How uncontrollable that snake is,' he said aloud, 'when the energy flows fully.' He turned the tap down a little. So far he felt nothing, though he knew the lawn was a webwork of forces underfoot, 'Otherwise the grass would not grow so green, nor the little stream run so full.' Perhaps he felt too serious; he shrugged his shoulders and wished he had a drink; mentally took one, and tried to feel in himself the relaxation it would bring him as it coursed down. He gripped the rods in their handles, and set out walking.

Oh, it was strong today! As he neared the site of the kitchen drain, down which the water was gushing from inside the house, the rods began to converge, pointing the way. He lifted his arms high to give them play, and they not only crossed as he passed over the drain, but began to swing back again to point straight back at him, as though his body itself were water, like a fountain jetting out of the pipe directly under his feet. He felt the force in his forearms, and he flung the rods clattering away from him and took out the hazel twig Matthew had used. Gripping the fork, his wrists seemed to glide upwards above the subterranean water, like birds volplaning over the land in a current of rising air. It was difficult to keep them down, it was difficult to resume walking. The twig rose and his hands lost hold of it, and spread outwards with the palms upwards, as if he were beseeching heaven. It was natural to stand there, like a welcoming figure, and let the force from the ground flow through him. His mind crowded with images, and there was a sudden power, and his arms swept round and clasped his body like a man hunched under a pelting shower from a thunderstorm, waiting for the lightning to strike. 'This is too much,' he said; 'it is my sensitivity enhanced without drink, I am losing control'; and the images were speeding so fast through his mind, like a great express-train made of water, the sides and windows all full of landscapes and people as though the water had taken visible impress of all it passed through, whether it was living tissue or river-bank, sky or rock, and in many of the living panes he saw hands unhappily washing themselves and the writing shapes of dirty clothes dancing away. 'Where shall I go to escape this power?' Where could he ever go — his ordinary screens were down — where could he ever go out of the reach of water? He was down on his knees now, and tumbling over and over down the slight slope, towards the big puddle made by the hose lying in the grass, and the little stream beyond. Suddenly he could resist it no longer, and it took him and stretched him out in the watery grass, where his body lay threshing, his head going from side to side like the nozzle of the hose with the full force of the mains pouring through it. The sinuous movement of his body took him down over the grass towards the bank of the little stream, and with a quick movement he flopped over the edge and fitted and flowed into the water's furrow like a tributary.

Millie had made a portion of shepherd's pie, some tinned peaches and cream, and a milky coffee last an hour and ten minutes while she read a book on Ancient Egypt, marvelling at the complex beliefs of this strange people. She saw that the elaborate edifice of funerary customs was analogous in some ways to the science she had been trained in: a vast experimental system made by a people who were not interested in quick results. In a way, she supposed, the results had been positive and affirmative: they sought immortality, and here was she, some thousands of years later, reading their elaborate communications. And taking what she herself needed from them. She was particularly interested in what she called 'brainstorms', by which she meant those sudden fits of 'otherness' — whether possession, prophecy, temporal lobe epilepsy, or artistic inspiration — that had taken hold of people from time to time in the world's history, and would always go on doing so, presumably; and which under various guises had been the chief subject of research of so many races: how to draw down the gods, how to become unlimited. Her own subject, experimental psychology, had become almost unsniffy about what it liked to call ASCs, meaning Altered States of Consciousness, and of course she was in the thick of it, what with the naive experiments of Matthew and Guy. Perhaps there would be something in what they were doing that would emerge as a paper; the dowsing was very remarkable. She thought that the clue to entering and leaving these states at will would be found in enduring the special conditions of this other form of consciousness without blanking out, perhaps by familiarising oneself with the inner representations of these states: by knowing the gods, since any condition which so seized the personality in its entirety would surely and naturally carry a personal quality to it, and could be called a 'god'. She had read of the 'integrating trance' and the 'still-interval trance' which were highly trained states in which these unfamiliar energies were put to use, brought back, as it were, and she hoped after further study to suggest certain techniques to Guy. She thought she should not attempt any training herself other than the kind she already possessed: trained observation. There was a certain sweetness in some breathing exercises she had read about and briefly tried which made her question this resolution, however. She wondered whether she should introduce simple hypnotic techniques into her home; she had a fantasy of Guy turned into a monster of potency and charm by means of a spinning disc that a figure of the goddess Isis would hold. She had just been reading of the Uraeus, that disc carried on the heads of all major Ancient Egyptian deities, which represented the full moon into whose silver round projected the upreared head of a snake. The snake was the hypnotiser *par excellence*, said the author, and this was a magnetic disc (as they called it then, she thought to herself, when they believed in mesmerism) that would throw people into a trance: spinning, the snake would appear to stand out against a flashing light, and (most interesting, this) its *meaning* was known to the subject, since the snake was the snake of the watery tides, and the sinuous processes of water itself, and the moon, the magnetiser, was the mistress of the tides. The result of knowing this was said to be the possession by the spirit of the snake, and, in the case of women in their menstrual courses, prophecy supervened, the blood sign of human fertility being held to be a special and extremely powerful instance of the presence of the serpent. She thought about her own period, and how her snake had in the last hour begun to shed its inner skin.

She unlocked the front door with her key, and wondered why the house was dark. Calling out for Guy, she went from room to room turning on the lights. As the electric light spread out from the kitchen window on to the lawn, she caught a large shadowy movement down by the old stream. She was a brave woman, and an observer, and it never occurred to her to be frightened by this. She found the kitchen door unlocked, and walked out into the garden, peering into the uncertain light. She could hear the little stream chugging away as she neared it, and felt the cool aura of running water. Then she heard a sudden running and hissing sound, and found herself enveloped by a part of the darkness, that felt cold and shaggy and wet, like the little stream itself. It bore her to the ground, and she felt water from the lawn seep through her blouse and cool her shoulder blades and spine. She felt her skirt pulled up, and the crotch of her pants pulled aside, and a vibrant warmness enter her, moving in a rhythm which was like a continuous flow rather than the gradually fusing strokes of the love-making she was used to with Guy. The flow gathered her own body into itself and she felt an unutterable sweetness pulling and pulling within her, and rising through her body into her throat. Ah! she could not breathe, it was like drowning under water in the smell of earth and water, she took breath but it was like steps one could only ascend, she inhaled but could not exhale, and brimmed so full of the water and the air that the wave must break, and it broke in a great cry which, far off, she realised was her own and another's.

She lay under the wet hulk of her attacker that was yet no more than a pleasant heaviness. Her whole skin felt as if joined by water to a mild source of electric current, from which it tingled, and this feeling went through her, and she realised she was exceedingly happy as she watched over the obscure shoulder the white disc of the full moon rise. 'I've been raped,' she thought, 'and whatever will Guy think. No wonder, it's the full moon. Thank God my period's started.' The breath of the monster fell across her cheek, and it rose from her and she got up too, and, reaching out for its slippery hand, she took it gently into the light. She knew it was Guy all along, really, which was why she had enjoyed herself so much; although he was nearly unrecognisable under all that mud and weed. She saw his smile, white in the stained face, and thought what a mess she herself must look, and this made her laugh. They went into the kitchen,

and she took newspapers from the boot cupboard for them to
undress on.

IV

DOWSER

I

He is too close: the changes are beginning.
Revivals, danced in the village street, be-antlered
Kill: the leg-bells beating, and the white shirts
And the living masks carved from budding trees,
The paper snakes winding about the dazzling shirtsleeves,
The linked swords in a net of steel, the dolorous blow
Delivered by every right hand . . . but a sudden fire
Got into the steel from sunshine, dazzled
The dancers, and the Morris shirt bled. Resting
In the garden of The Cricketers, I idly watch
The eleven domestic blooms wrapped in blinding white
With, leaking between the petals, blood-red pollen;
I watch the thrush bounding and trotting fast
Off the hot flagstones into the earthy shadows
And as it passes the sunpatch, like a penknife blade
The beak glints; in the stone, like linked swords
The quartz rays gleam, and in every boulder of dust.

While in the hazy distance, the Dowser glitters.
I think the water is rising in arcades around him,
That he is the wandering centre of a park
Of fountains that bow to him, of steely streams
Like linked swords, and white falls, and clouds
Like bleached oaks that follow.
This man must not come too close to my farm.
The timber would bud, the harvest
Rot in green conflagration.

2

The grasses hiss on their note, are blades whetted with water.
The trees are plump with sap, their every shadow moist.
He walks with hands clasped as through water-caves
Deep underground, he walks through torrents
That are far below, head bent. Beneath,
The bedrock cracks and shrills with crystalline rock-sap
Of water that speeds through greensand counties,
Over shires of clay and swift slate, like trains
That are all windows, like tankers

Of glass, transporting glass, like glass dining cars
Full of wet drinkers holding their glasses high.
At the surface, among the sunlit moistures,
The leathery dowser unclasps his hands, 'Here,'
He says, 'about twenty feet down,'

Where the thunderstorm leaps through its nether home
Or lies as water petals folded in one abyssal bloom.

'Is that automatic writing?' teased Millie, when Guy showed her the poem about the Dowser.

'By no means,' said Guy seriously. 'I think the Dowser might be a very dangerous functionary, and would make customs wobble. The idea of the sword-dance is like the converse of the firing-squad: the officer loads all the rifles with blanks except one, and nobody but he knows which one that is. All the men shoot at their comrade, but only one is the murderer.'

'The guilt spreads thin.'

'Usually the experience marks all the men for the rest of their lives. A lot of men were shot by their fellow soldiers after the mutinies at Passchendaele in the First World War. A famous dance-leader who died in his seventies the other day left a confession and a description of how he was tormented all his life by taking part in a firing-squad. In the sword-dance you link the blades so that everybody kills, and if one hand should hold back, that would not prevent the sacrifice. In those days blood was spilled at the solstice for the benefit of all. Cricketers are a kind of Morris man, with willow wands instead of swords.'

'With the blooms in the pub yard, that would be the vernal equinox.'

'Oh, I can't help that. All the festivals get moved about. My point was that the presence of certain kinds of people made others accident-prone, and perception altered, so you could see the sword-dance in every rolling grain of dust. Nobody in a conservative village would welcome this.'

'So the festivals would be to keep the forces at bay, or encapsulated, rather than to arouse them.'

'Certainly. The planchette is rather like the linked swords. Nobody can tell which of us is writing.'

Their fingers were laid lightly on the edges of the little board that rolled on its castors between them, the pencil fixed in it scratching zig-zags on the sheet of smooth white wallpaper they had spread over the table.

'Nobody's writing at present. Let's go on talking; with nonchalance, of course. Something will happen.'

'We ought to think of bees.'

The board twitched and ran across the paper.

'Keep thinking of bees. I will follow you, Millie. Tell me your pictures.'

'I'm thinking of a bee-swarm clustered like thick grapes on a bough. The bough is three times its normal thickness with bees, but as light as air, since all their wings are hovering. I can hear the great buzz of their standing flight; it covers every pitch in one, it is higher than I can hear and lower too, but it is not loud. All the cells of my body seem to hum in sympathy with this sound, as if they were cells of the comb, and my blood was bees tending the cells.'

The two were silent now in the dim light of the covered lamp, and the planchette board raced. Millie's breathing had grown shallow and regular; she was evidently in a light trance. Guy allowed his mind to roam as it would, but gently pulling it back whenever he noticed that it had left the sound or form of bees. The sensations of his dowsing experiment came back into his skin, and with it he seemed to look down into the earth and its rock, which was honeycombed with cells and channels, all full of sweet water humming with its passage through the stone. In the graveyard he saw the dead wrapped like pupae, bandaged and blue like the Ushabti figure, and as he watched he saw some of the bindings burst, and winged creatures struggling within the narrow tomb. He saw, and heard, a swarm of bees pour inexhaustibly from the trunk of a hollow tree great as a sequoia, the honey-swarm vacating its white hexagonal skeleton, and rise over the land like a great snake rearing high over the forest, and he watched the individual insects volplaning in the hot climbing air-currents, ascending through mists and clouds, and drinking the diluted nectar of the clouds, which had arisen from banks of flowers. He saw a toga'ed Arcadian bee-master, good shepherd leading his bee-flocks through all the flowers appropriate to the season of the year, through the coconut-smelling furze at the springtime, the flowers winged like the bees that entered them, like little suns, and through the musty hanging swatches of ivy at the year's end. This bee-master had learnt to lead his swarms by humming to them. Guy saw a red crystal bee that was a great sunset-cloud made of shattered ice let down its proboscis of rain into all the flowers at once, and their nectars flowed away under the ground into one great tumultuous river pouring through the earth that smelt of flowers. Then he saw the first great swarm flying back into its sequoia trunk that must have been a stem of honeycomb under the bark two hundred feet high, the black snake of bees coiling round and round the trunk, and being swallowed up in the tree as the hum in his mind grew less, and he woke to the lamplight again, his eyes having been open all this time, and staring without sight at the planchette that had now ceased its motion. Millie, still with fingertips on the board, looked at him a little slyly. The paper was covered with designs.

Millie had been discomposed by this session, had been shocked out of her role as pure observer. She explained a little bashfully that she had just had another orgasm, rather like the one she had with the mud boltered Guy, Guy 'as the river Scamander', in the garden, when she had made love with the river. Millie's orgasm that had made her shout, or, rather, sing out, was a new sensation to her, and it had left her admirably satisfied, she said, so that she wouldn't mind, really, living the rest of her life with the memory of that orgasm: even if no other came up to it again. But it had, and just now, for the first one had left her with a hair-trigger. Some channel had been opened, and the little scratching of the planchette, with the bee-hum that she had imagined, had spun her along the corridors of this remarkable feeling. There was the sense of intimacy with Guy too, and an exploration with him; all produced this second superb but quieter spasm. She wondered if she had cried out aloud. Guy had been sunk in his own reverie, and could not tell. She thought she had been changed utterly. Guy had been changed for her too: it was that she now saw him not just as plain old Guy, playful and interesting and sincere though he might be, but rather like the mask of a power, or the crest of an extremely powerful wave that came from beyond Guy, holding in front of it, as it were, his face and body. Yet it was still Guy, and he had always been this; as, she supposed, she was always Millie. Now, in their course of study — which was theirs now, and not his alone — they were faced with their first written communication. If it was writing. The centre of the paper, where the planchette had rested to begin with, was covered with little Z shaped marks. These clustered close together, making a shaded area: both realised that one could see the ZZZZZZZ as the sound of a swarm, in its black clustering together. Millie felt this was no more than a coincidence, though she thought it pretty.

Then there was a swooping mark of the pencil up to the top right hand corner of the paper, where the movement of the planchette had rounded a smallish circle. This circle was not continuous with the path the pencil had left, but was separated, leaving a gap, and Millie felt puzzled by this fact. It surely meant that the planchette had, by some means, jumped off the paper to do this drawing. The circle was surrounded by longish bristling strokes, and the board must have had to jump to score each of these also. Their fingers must have moved to tilt the planchette sufficiently to lift the pencil off the paper at these points, but this must show an extraordinary degree of unconscious control.

Then the design moved to the left hand side of the sheet, and down this were drawn fat leaning figures of eight. There were five of them. The eights were more of the shape of cottage-loaves, with a fat circle flattened on another fat circle. Where the circles met was an undulating line, and Millie noticed that this had five peaks also: the same number as there were figures of eight. These undulating centre-lines, and the eights to which they belonged, were all tilted at the same angle.

'I expected writing,' said Guy.

'You can't have everything at once,' said Millie, 'and these remind me of something I saw long long ago.'

'Eight, symbol of eternity, intersection of the two worlds, ogdoad, figure of completion . . .'

'I'm afraid, Guy, it was nothing so vague as that.' With a delighted shout she ran to the bookcase and picked out a volume of the encyclopaedia. She riffled the pages, and put it down opened in front of Guy. There on the page was their design. It was a bee-dance.

The encyclopaedia told them that bees were able to communicate to the rest of the hive the location of the best sources of nectar and pollen by tracing out a dance on the vertical sides of the comb. For distances over a hundred yards, the 'wagtail' dance was used: figures of eight with a wobbly middle-line. The angle of this mid-line to the position of the sun indicated the direction of the food-source; and the distance was given by the number of dances, the frequency and duration of a buzz that the bee gave during the mid-line run, and the time it took to trace the whole figure. While it was dancing, the bee would hand out samples of nectar or pollen to the spectator-bees, who, after watching, were able to find the source of those samples by themselves. Guy and Millie supposed that the undulations of the mid-line would have to stand for these indications, especially as the number of figures was the same as the number of undulations. 'Which can't be a coincidence,' said Guy; 'Not if it means anything at all,' agreed Millie.

Perhaps five miles made a good beginning. The sun was just setting as they had sat down for their seance, and all the mid-lines were inclined at an angle of 32 degrees to the sun — as the smallish circle with bristling rays must be — drawn on the wallpaper sheet. They got the local map out, and a protractor and a ruler, and drew a line 32 degrees east of west, as the drawing indicated. They marked off five miles on the one-inch map. The line passed straight through David's Institute, and it was exactly five miles away from their home.

They began to worry about Matthew. He had left that early summer dowsing afternoon with Meave, and it was now autumn. Millie called at the Institute once or twice, after finding that he had moved out from his digs. The first time she had gone with piles of mail, mostly circulars, as Matthew had not bothered to have his post redirected.

The Institute was a big, old house on the outskirts of the town, with a large and neglected garden, and a brass plate screwed to an outer gatepost which merely said: 'The Institute for Study: Callers by Appointment.' She had seen courses and lectures advertised in the local paper, so it wasn't as remote or exclusive as this posh shingle suggested. She walked up the drive to the front door and looked for a bell-push. To her amusement there was only a large old bell-*pull*. She tugged the dull, greeny brass knob, which came out about three inches on its wire, and heard a bell jangle in the distance. She waited ten minutes, and when nobody came she put the letters in the box and left.

The second time was more productive. She went up the day after the bee-dance communication. She wanted to see Matthew, or hear something about him, and she was also curious about being directed there by the planchette. The door was answered this time by a rather attractive man. He was a little taller than she was, and wore a spotless white roll neck pullover, which suited his slender figure. He had a square chin and jaw, and a large mouth with very mobile and red lips. When he smiled politely, as he did now, his mouth was bracketed pleasantly with deep lines, though his eyes were still and watchful, without laughter marks. This made a contradiction in his face: the pleasant sociable lower half, and the shining and watchful eyes, which seemed as black as pitch. His hair was also very dark, and of medium length, rather heavy and curling round a high and creamy brow. The lofting of his forehead was quite beautiful, and she thought how striking it would have been on a girl. The skin was pure and transparent, and the reflection of light from his sweater probably emphasised this, but she could see as she hesitated before speaking a play of

75

colours, very light and very subtle, within the flesh of the face, as if the skin, usually so pigmented or rough in most people as to conceal this, in him revealed the play of red and blue, made the lightest of pastel shades, that were the responses below the skin of the minute arterioles and venules and capillaries to emotion and environment. There was no shadow of beard. She wondered what would make him blush, what would make him blanch. This interplay of colours, she knew, was one of the valued qualities of a model posing in the nude: and a painter would stand entranced at the change of texture and colour in his subject as he spoke to her, praised her for her pose, or scolded her. She felt a small and deep sexual pang in regarding this skin, which worried her a little: she found many men sexually interesting, but this was so distant and yet so definite, as though if it were to come closer up it might be too decided by far, even irresistible. Still, she wondered whether she would not have been wiser to turn away at once, since that little pang was fear as well as sexuality. She felt she must be cautious, now she had this 'hair-trigger', having slept with the river, like a god.

In the event she was courageous. 'Hello,' she said, 'I'm a friend of Matthew's. My name's Millie. I'd like to know how he is. Can I see him?'

'Millie! I'm very pleased to see you. Matthew has spoken of you and Guy a great deal. I'm afraid that everybody's out just now. David is away at a conference, and Meave has taken Matthew and the twins for a drive. Would you like to come in a moment? I can tell you all about him. I'm Simon.'

He stood aside, and ushered her through the gloomy hall. The floor was covered with a flowered carpet that was thick-piled, but threadbare in odd places, under the hall table, behind a hatstand, as though it had been turned around after much heavy wear. Simon opened a dark mahogany door on a glare of white.

It was a white-painted room leading on to a conservatory. The walls, the ceiling and the floor were painted dead white, and there were sheepskin rugs that must have been specially washed and bleached to look dazzling. She looked down at her dusty shoes ruefully, but Simon smiled and gestured to her not to worry. The conservatory was separated from the room itself by glass doors, the frames of which were also entirely white; every strut of every pane of the glass roof and walls was immaculately so. There were shutters above eye-level, fastened outside the glass, and they were white. Light poured in from the roof, and she could see blue sky and the tops of trees. She turned round. There was a sheet of thick glass which served as a table, on white painted cast iron legs, and by it were two white wooden kitchen chairs, gate-backed. Simon asked her to sit down.

'What a remarkable room,' she said. 'Do you use it for some special study?' She thought it looked like a white spiderweb of thick cables, all their natural light and transparency sucked out of them.

'I suppose it does look like a clinic. We're not that, you know, only a Society.'

'A Society dedicated to giving up drink in favour of mediumship?'

He laughed loudly, with an unpleasant bray. He became animal: his red lips lifted from teeth that were too well-built and too yellow. She thought that the lines on either side of his mouth that had seemed attractive to her were strain-lines: they had been produced by setting his expression so that it would smile and not laugh, and the teeth not be revealed. This meant that he was concerned to control a part of his nature that at usual times he managed to wrestle into the image of himself that he preferred. There was no easy transition from one side of his nature to another, she suspected. The teeth and the jaw and the mouth were all strong in themselves, and though well-developed, no deformity. It was that he stabled that other expression under a mask of charm. He kept a nightmare, that whinnied. What would he look like at a party, where the host would be laughing with his drinkers? A sort of goat, perhaps, wearing a man's cranium like a tall, beautifully modelled bowler.

'Dedicated to that, among other things. You would be pleased at Matthew, Millie. He has drunk nothing but water since he came here.'

'The water we gave him had quite a kick. Did you hear about that?'

'Yes, of course. It was a central experience for him.'

77

'Are you his doctor?'

'I? Certainly not. It's more that he is mine.'

'What do you mean?'

'He is a very clear man, Millie, there is no guile. It does us all good to have him here.'

'I wish I could see him.'

'He has said himself that he wants to complete his course of training.'

'Training. Do you think of bees here?' She smiled, to show that she was not trying to be offensive. She would have liked to insult this man and leave, but she wanted to know as much as she could first. She was annoyed at the little filament of sexual desire for him that flickered in her.

'We find thinking of bees a very productive exercise. We have hives here. David likes to eat hive products, honey, royal jelly, propolis. He likes his tables polished with beeswax. We have recordings of the hive that we use for meditation. David has a gift. He can hypnotise the bees. He can sing so that the hives go quiet and listen to him.'

'I don't believe you.' She was cross. 'My own training was in psychology. I'm a scientist. I would have to record phenomena like this under my own conditions.'

'I'm not asking you to believe me, dear Millie.' His laugh and his smile were too strong. 'Except that I would like you to understand that your friend is well, and has probably never been better. Drinking concealed his abilities. He is finding new interests in life and new skills, and we hope he will stay with our community since he could bring much to it.'

'Has he become a medium?'

'A very remarkable one.'

'Couldn't I see him at work?'

'One day, certainly. He will doubtless give public readings.'

'Simon, tell me what mediumship is. Do you know something special about it here?'

'We each of us have our various sensitivities, which develop differently in each person. David is a doctor, and in his doctoring he employs what you might call mediumistic faculties. He sees important things about his patients fleetingly, and he has learnt to catch such intuitions out of the air. Matthew's mediumship began in his poetry; and poetry is a help. It gives the medium pace, consistency, imagery in his rapid talk, and this poetic talking can raise up the sensitivities of his listeners so that their intuitions run parallel with the ones he is showing them. There is a snowballing effect.'

'With possession? Does his audience become possessed?'

'If that's what you like to call it. We prefer to call it "enthusiasm", and it is to give form to the energies that are at present beyond our conscious control that we study the wholesome animals.'

'I hope your bees never become wasps.'

'Indeed,' murmured Simon.

'And what of yourself, Simon? And Meave? What are your sensitivities?'

'We are sexual, Millie.'

The room went a little wobbly and unreal for a moment, as her mind shied away from what Simon had said. He was looking at her with his troubling face.

'We know how to present ourselves, Millie, to keep people interested.'

She saw that the way his mouth played with the human charm over the animal bone was grossly sexual, and so was the depth of his skin's pastel and light. His teeth were not vegetarian, like the horse she had first thought of, but wolfish, tigerish. There was a glint of red in his eye, as though he were angry. The modelling of his brow was exquisite, and there was a slight flush in the flawless skin. She saw the thick line of his erection in the tight denim trousers, and her eyes flicked away.

'We believe that sexuality is the free energy that, controlled, becomes mediumship. We are mediums because of our sexuality.'

'And Matthew is Meave's sexual partner?'

'He is partner with both of us, Millie. We are twins. We are complementary to both sides of him. Matthew needs to become a man-woman, like David, to fulfil his greatness. Meave's children are twins too. There should always be this partnership of twins available to the students of sex here. Sex is the light of the body, it is twinned in each of us, and it must not be hidden. It is the Kingdom on earth.'

Millie had risen, and turned away from him, towards the door. Closing her ears mentally against Simon's murmur, she walked firmly out of the room, down the hall, and out of the front door, into the open air. Simon did not pursue her out of the house. She heard the front door close with a snap. This made her crosser still, so that she almost forgot Matthew; not just that day, but for several weeks, which melted into months.

V

In those months, as though the antagonistic meeting at the Institute had given Guy and Millie a push, their work sped ahead. They reasoned that Matthew would get in touch when he wanted to; that he was in a doctor's care; they had their own work to do; and when it was time for Matthew to declare himself, if he had become a great medium of some sort, then their own exercises would have sharpened their discrimination when they met again. Then they wouldn't mind studying under him, or learning from him; though nobody, Millie said, would get her back to that Institute, Slippery Simon, or to meet that horrible pair of twins. All Guy had to do now was to think of water running, and to compose some picture containing favourite elements that would send him into his reverie with the water, for him to melt away into trance: the water breaking over a fall, and the drops flying, and a smooth backward tuck of the stream gathered round a stone, and bees alighting there to drink, their reflections flying upwards and meeting them in the water — this was one. There was now no need for the planchette. If he settled himself to think in this way with a pencil loosely gripped in his left hand (he was ordinarily right-handed) then the pencil would start to run over the paper almost before he had formed his mental picture. They found big sheets of smooth wallpaper laid across the table best, since the communicators followed no margins narrower than the reach of their medium's arm. Millie was supposed to watch and keep notes, but the sight of Guy's fingers running over the page, and the writing pouring out, gave her her own picture of the mighty stream with Guy's face that was more than Guy. So that far from being the observer now, she was participant, falling into her own trance, the natural finale of which was an orgasm of the kind she had newly learnt. Her sight would clear to see the page filled with writing, and Guy exhausted, in his sweat. It was a strange congress, and the seance room was like a marriage bed, and the dreams were written on the great off-white sheets. But what was the worth of these fragmentary speeches, raving, exhortations that went on as they slept? Until the mad bomber spoke through Guy's carpenter's pencil they could not guess.

Guy lost weight and seemed much fitter. There was no drinking. The communications contained many voices, were fluent and broken. Millie had just started a cross-index of themes and apparent personalities when Guy's first full communication came, and shook him to pieces. *I did not make the bombs myself, though I took the terrorist handbook to Little Sean, as we call him . . .* and rapidly on the heels of this, Guy mixing his sustaining honey-and-water, the phone call from Matthew, and then Matthew himself in flight from the Institute, white and shaking, as though he had never been away: *I was born to suffer what I myself did just like everyone around me and I get to my feet and I shout out to them all 'Stop!' and all their reflections freeze in the mirrors and in one second from now all the hearts in the room will burst.*

'I was in that place, Guy, and I almost saw the face of the bomber before light started coming from the haversack beside her and I got such a jolt that I remembered nothing until I was able to read the script.'

'Will you look at ours now?' said Guy. 'Are you well enough?'

'I've been through it, you know. I doubt whether you could show me anything I've not guessed.' There was a touch of arrogance in his new manner; Groucho had gone. Guy put his half of the communication in front of Matthew, and the two read silently together.

Matthew lit a cigarette, and looked around him in the old way, as though he needed a pull on some alcohol or other before a word would issue from him. He said, 'They swarm like bees, you understand. You will swarm like fragments of yourself when you are dead, and so shall I. The ghost comes out of the body like a swarm of bees, and the air is cold, and many of us die at its touch. We try to put the ghosts together at the Institute, you know,' he giggled, 'but they keep coming apart. I had Groucho there once' — he rolled his eyes and stuck his cigarette in his mouth as though it were a big cigar — 'but he kept on breaking up. David thinks that since the Queen's sexual exudations and vapours keep the hive together, then if we all have lots of sex over there, that will help the ghosts. That's why he has that awful pair. They won't leave me alone. David wants us to round ourselves into a composite mind, so that we shall never be out of touch even when he dies, or one of us dies, but they're quite mad, the lot of them. Or so I thought: now we've got something real or halfway real; I came to you because I almost recognised the bomber and it frightened me and I knew they never help you up there if you're frightened; they think the sexual embrace is the solution to all problems. But what you've shown me is worse. It may be that the evil people survive, even though they've been blown to pieces. Somewhere that pub is still flying apart, humming and buzzing with sharp fragments of glass like innumerable stings, a great splash of blood expanding like a cloud. The thoughts go on and go on for ever, and you think it's inspiration, but it's incitement to murder. I talked to Brahms, you know: he had given up music and was writing poetry and studying economics. He gave tips for races and advised David on shares. It was mediocre advice; we lost nothing, gained nothing. Deep inside I don't want to go back, Millie, but it's a drug stronger than drink. The whole place smells of that filthy beeswax. I can't do without my nookie at all, you know. It's as bad as alcohol and has got a kick like a horse' — the Groucho manner touched him here. 'Millie and Guy, we've done what we set out to do: given up drink; both of us. I think we are all of us wrong if we accept anything but depth. I should have given up drink to write poetry; not to become some kind of a guru. My only answer to a naughty bomber is to write the poem that shows her face. If I write it well enough, then, maybe, she will not want to destroy it. I put down what has happened to me like a play. I want you to have it; it makes more sense than those scrawls we've all been doing, even this one.' He pointed to the closely written sheets of wallpaper. 'The play's in here.' He took an envelope out of his poacher's pocket. 'It's all true in its way,' he said, 'done properly it'd be a nice Punch and Judy to divert the children. Spirits exist, you know, but there are not as many as we think. David has made the bees swarm and we'll all get stung.' He passed an envelope over the table to Millie who was staring at him with wide eyes. Then Matthew got up, his cigarette cocked in his mouth, and fanned them a farewell greeting as with the pudgy hands of F. Z. ('Cuddles') Zakor, Hollywood comedian, player of exasperated show-biz impresarios, dead and buried in black-and-white celluloid these many years past.

VI

Guy went out to the door with his hand on Matthew's shoulder. When he came back, Millie was gazing at the envelope, which she had put in the centre of the great round seance table. 'Millie?' he said softly. She was in a trance, or reverie. Slowly her fingers came forward and lightly touched the envelope as she would the planchette, with a firm expectancy. Guy moved round the table and saw that her eyes were open, and staring into the shadows at the other side of the room. As he watched, tears gathered in them, and ran down her face; now she was like a child crying, and the tears *spurted* from her eyes.

'Poor, poor Matthew,' she said; 'we should have got him away from those people. I can feel tears in this envelope. It is a terrible house.'

'It's not too late,' said Guy quickly, 'I can run and get him back. I can persuade him somehow. He can't have gone far.'

'I don't think you'll find him,' said Millie.

Guy went back to the front door and unbolted it, and looked up and down the street. It was raining lightly. The street shone with its lamps, and Guy could see the length of it in either direction. There was no sign of Matthew. Guy could not understand how he could have got out of sight so quickly. He went back inside.

Millie had woken from her reverie, had the envelope in her hand. 'You'd better read it, Guy.'

He took it; it was sealed. 'Don't you want to know what's inside, Millie?'

She looked surprised as he tore the flap. 'Isn't it open? I was reading it just now. It's a play.'

Guy took the dozen or so sheets of paper out and looked at them. 'I expect Matthew's all right,' he said; 'he was shaken a bit, but then so were we. He looked careworn, but OK.'

'I don't think that was Matthew,' she said.

Chapter four

Finding a ghost

I

This is the text of the play Guy found in Matthew's envelope:

FINDING A GHOST

Dramatis personae: Protagonist; 2 human or earthly Helpers; 2 Spirit-clowns.

(Stage with table and chairs. Downstage, the Magic Theatre. This is a 'black theatre'; a small proscenium framed with electric light bulbs and draped inside with black curtains. There is no need for a perfect illusion, but actors dressed or draped in black can, by merging against the drapes, seem to appear or disappear. Objects they carry will appear to float.

The Magic Theatre acts as a feed-back device operated by the Spirit-clowns. It gives back versions of the truth to the human actors of the story, who respond to it or not according to their various abilities.

To begin with, the setting is quiet and empty. Suddenly an immense figure trots on to the stage, half running, half waddling. It is composed of the two Spiritclowns, one on the other's shoulders, draped in a long ulster. The figure runs over the stage, making grimaces at the audience, then whisks behind the Magic Theatre façade. The lights of the Magic Theatre go on for a bit, then off again. There is a pause. The Magic Theatre is charged up and waiting. Enter Protagonist.)

Protagonist: Good evening. I want to tell you I have lost my faith. No, I'm not here to preach you a sermon. It's just that there's — nothing! You're sitting here, waiting for an illusion, a device of the theatre. I'm telling you it's all an illusion. You came here through painted scenery; a big river painted, big buildings beyond.

A few cranes. Somerset House, full of paper. Some gardens. A concrete set called the South Bank, the National Theatre. Masks. An accidental planet whirling around an accidental star, backdrop upon backdrop of accidental stars, veil upon veil. Whisk the veil away — pouf! nothing. The sun goes out, we go out. A neutron bomb goes off over Big Ben -just over there *(points)* — with its glare like a sun, and its rays penetrate walls like glass. You flow down over these seats like a slippery waterfall of grilled cheese. The scene is shifted-transformation!

We're all in this together. So what I say for myself goes for you too. None of you really believes there is anything. No, really! I am a modern man speaking to modern men and women. You do as you like: lie, murder, cheat — there's nothing and nobody, no big Nobodaddy in the sky to stop you. Faith is something lost on one of the big battlefields, among all the broken metal. Or it went down in the Titanic. Or Luther argued it away. Any excuse!

We're like Faust. We'll sell our souls to get what we want. Except that science has sold them for us, and we've nothing to bargain with any more, and nobody to bargain with either. We've got the nothing we never asked for.

(While he is speaking, Spirit-clowns dressed as dogs have sidled out of the Magic Theatre, close up to him. He absently strokes them as he is talking, without really paying attention to what he is doing. After a bit, the dogs gambol back, making distinct motions of courtship and copulation as they disappear behind the scenes.)

A modern man speaking to modern men and women. I'm sure I do speak for everybody here when I say that we have not lost our appetite for marvels. We still want there to be something. I

86

think we don't really care whether it is an illusion or not, so long as it is a grand illusion. We go from guru to guru, from sham to shaman, from confidence man to hypnotist to magician to new wave priest to megalithic stone circles to tantric yoga to Tai-Chi to alchemy to Jungian psychology — and all the way back again via dowsing and animal magnetism. Well, as I told you, I share this. I am going to tell you the story of *my* search for the one little grain of true nonsense I could believe in. More — I am going to share it with you and show it to you. Showing it to you, I am really asking you a big question. You'll see how I became a spiritualist, and sought final answers. Then I became a black-magic practitioner, and the prize I got there was a nervous breakdown. Naturally that turned me into an analysand, and I sought my answers from a psychoanalyst. The psychoanalyst couldn't believe his luck, and so he incontinently hypnotised me. I didn't care for this, but somehow it made me a poet. Yes a poet. And since the only good poets are dead ones, it became incumbent on me to die. And as I died I saw something. And I have come back here on to this stage to show the whole story, and to show you what I saw at the end of it, and to ask you, my peers, the big question, whether what I saw at the end was true.

(Black-out to light bulbs only of the Magic Theatre. Stage lights slowly up as the two Human Helpers, respectably dressed, one as Medium, the other as Presenter, come on and sit at table expectantly. Protagonist is standing outside circle of light watching them; he makes as if knocking on door, entering house, giving hat and coat to maid, entering seance room.)

Presenter: Good evening, Mr Matthew. How very good of you to come. This is the Medium, Mrs Drudge. The atmosphere is most propitious tonight. You shall have the communication you desire from the world of the spirits. You have an excellent aura. Please sit down. It will not be long before the Medium goes into her trance.

(The Medium breathes very heavily, and the bulbs on the Magic Theatre fade and brighten in her breathing rhythm. Then they shine steadily, and the Medium sits bolt-upright, staring straight at the black curtains.)

Medium: Oh. Oh. I cannot see. It is so dark. So dark in the centre. I must go down, down, into the darkness. So sable, such a dazzling darkness. I cannot see in this bright darkness. My spirit is blind. I am falling, falling into the blindness.

(While the Medium is speaking, the curtains of the Magic Theatre twitch and on comes one of the Spirit-clowns. She is in black, except for white face and hands, and she carries a small conjurer's table and a basket containing several objects. She stares out of the proscenium frame directly at the Medium, her stretched hand above her eyes, like a sailor searching out a horizon. She mimes exasperation at the Medium's blindness, picks an electric torch out of the basket and shines it on the Medium's face.)

Oh, I can see! I have fallen into the light. It is so bright down here. Brighter than the sun. It is bright with the bodies of all the spirits that are thronging forward in the radiant brightness.

(At this 'all the spirits' the second Spirit-clown comes on, also in white-face and white-hands. The two spirits float their faces and hands about.)

I must ask the spirits where is Red Star. Where is Red Star, my Indian Guide? Tell Red Star I am here.

(One Spirit-clown picks a feather headdress out of the basket and puts it on the other's head. Also a wampum Indian-style waistcoat, which she helps the other into, clothing the black space below face with the help of busy white hands.)

> Hello, Red Star. I am very glad to see you at last. There is much power here today. But you are here and all is well. This is Mr Matthew, a seeker after truth, who has come to speak to you. Do you not think his aura is a good one?

(The Medium now changes voice and speaks in Red Star's voice, but the Spirit-clown mimes bombastically what she says with his lips and actions.)

> How! Heap big power here to-day, Missus. Your friend want know about Summerland where we spirits live? The sun shine all the time. We live by cliffs dazzling as the white clouds in the sky. Our houses are built by our minds. We clothe ourselves in our thoughts. You want big cigar? Big cigar there at once, at your command: thought-form. You want woman? You want to be woman? A thought will do it. Everything is thought-form, even in your world. But we know it here. We form, transform. Your world is made of thoughts of Great Spirit, and he think solid and slow. You run around inside his mind, like quick thoughts among the slow ones. Here, we spirits are trying to be like Great Spirit, practise making all the good things, sunshine and white cliffs, dazzling sands, big cigars and women.

Presenter (whispers to Protagonist):

> Is there any person you wish to contact in the afterlife? Any question you wish to ask? Red Star is a very advanced spirit and can tell you what you need to know.

Protagonist: Yes. Yes. I had a son who died. It was some while back. Some years. When we were young. His mother and I were young together.

(One of the Spirit-clowns slips out of the Magic Theatre and puts a bunch of brightly coloured flowers on the table. The Helper looks straight at it without seeing it, then sees it and jumps, laying his hand on the Medium's arm. She is still looking bolt-forward. The Protagonist notices the flowers. The Helper is made uneasy by the appearance of the flowers.)

These flowers. Where did these lovely flowers come from? They weren't on the table before. They smell as fresh as if they had just been picked.

Presenter: Oh, sometimes that happens. I don't know . . . it is propitious. I will ask the Medium when she wakens.

Protagonist: You sound frightened.

Presenter: No, no. It is just one of those things that sometimes happen. It means good luck. It is an earnest of life from the other world. It is called an apport. There are more important things. You came here to ask about your son.

Medium: So many spirits thronging. Some with baby-faces, some with beards. Tell me, Red Star, is our guest's son with you, in those bright regions? Here come the young people in a cloud of shining faces.

Presenter: Your son was dark, was he not? His hair was fair? And he was tall, I'm sure.

Protagonist: Oh, no, that wouldn't be right, would it. You could make up something to fit the description!

Presenter: Hush, sir! The Medium is in a trance.

Medium: I see a spirit coming. He is young, tall and fair. He is beauty himself. The asphodel springs in his footsteps.

Presenter: Is this your son, sir? He was quite tall, I think.

Protagonist: No, as a matter of fact he was short. He had a slight club-foot. His skin was fair though.

Medium: The little golden-haired spirit is saying something to me. Quick, I can't quite hear. Red Star, what does he say? *(In Red Star's voice.)* No Club Foot here. We teachum healing. All bodies perfect. Your son loves you, Mr Matthew, and will always love you.

Protagonist: Anyone could say that. How do I know who it is? Platitudes and sentimentalities. Give me his true name and I will believe you.

Presenter: You must not be sceptical. It will break the influence.

Medium: I see a J and a T.

Protagonist: Yes, one of his names did have a J in it. What a banality!

(After the apport, the Spirit-clown has slipped back on to the Magic Theatre area. During the prevarication about the appearance of Matthew's son, and his name, the spirits have been miming youth, age, tallness, shortness, have put on dark wigs and fair wigs, have pulled out big written letters T and J. Now, as the Protagonist is obviously getting fed up, one Spirit-clown pulls a microphone out of the basket, unwinds its cord, switches it on, and utters the name into it. Speakers in the auditorium boom out the name.)

Spirit:	JOHNNIE! JOHNNIE! JOHNNIE!
Protagonist:	Yes! that was his name. Oh, Johnnie, where are you? Where have you gone? Why do you sound like that?
Spirit:	Burning. Burning. Burning. I am in Hell, Father. I am in Hell burning. Burning with all the others like me. Burning. Burning.
Protagonist:	Oh, dear God, what is this! Whose is this voice? *(Turning to Medium.)* What do you mean? What have you done?

(Medium goes into convulsions. Spirits hurriedly pack up gear and disappear behind scenes. Lights on Magic Theatre go out.)

Presenter:	You must not speak to the Medium while she is in trance. Look what you have done. She must have a glass of water. Please. Let me pass.
Protagonist:	But the voice. Didn't you hear the voice? Tell me about the voice. I must know if that was my son. *(Weeps.)*

(But the two Spiritualists pay him no attention. The Presenter fusses over the Medium, and gently gets her to walk off stage. Protagonist is left watching them go. Pause. Then he shrugs his shoulders, and turns and addresses the audience.)

As you saw, my first venture into the realms of truth was a disaster. And what could that big voice have been, except truth? I decided that if my poor son was burning in Hell, then I might as well be reunited with him in due course, and in the meanwhile draw on the energies, powers and pleasures of Hell, and enjoy myself, as Faust did. Did Blake not tell us how he walked among the fires of Hell, and how he was delighted there with the enjoyments of genius, which to angels look like torment and insanity? Very well then, I would become a genius, by the grace of Hell. My Johnnie was not really *suffering* there. His voice was big with a superabundance of Energy. My course was clear. I would study black magic, and become my true self before death overtook me, as it must overtake us all.

(Magic Theatre lights up. Helpers walk on to front stage in robes, carrying various implements, including two magic circles cut out of cloth, which they lay on stage. The bigger circle is laid for the conjuring Helper-adept, the smaller one is for the Protagonist.)

Do you think that all this play-acting will help us? Why these trappings? Why do you lay that circle?

Adept: To find a centre. Will you please stand here? The smaller circle is for your protection.

Protagonist: I will do anything you say.

Adept: Occide canem.

Protagonist: You told me I must do a ridiculous cruel thing if I was to see the truth. I killed the puppy-dog and here is its blood, but I felt sick in my heart.

Adept: You must feel sickness and helplessness before you can see again as a child sees, or as a man with a mortal sickness sees, clear yet tremulously, clear and with infinite feeling. *Occide infantem.*

Protagonist: Kill a child? Is that how you get a double-allowance of souls for Hell? That I should tempt the child to its naughtiness, and then kill it: you will have the child and its murderer then. I'm afraid that you will have to show that you are competent guides before I go so far. I might simply be putting my soul in your hands, for blackmail. The dog will have to be enough for the time being. *(Hands him a phial.)*

Adept: Very well. I cannot guarantee that you will see anything at all. But I will make the conjuration. Assuredly *I* will see the result of my prayers and ritual, as I have gone through sickness upon sickness and have found the truth.

Protagonist: Which is?

Adept: Those who restrain desire, do so because theirs is weak enough to be restrained. Now, after I have made this conjuration you must stand strictly within the circle. To go outside it is to risk death.

Protagonist: *Occide adeptum.*

Adept: You will not jest if you can look into the depths that I will cut open for you with this sword.

(Adept stands in circle and facing audience at first takes phial of blood and uncorks it. He pours some of the 'blood' in the palm of his hand and rubs it over his forehead and face. He tears open his robe and rubs the blood over his throat and upper chest.)

O Lucifer, light-bearer, true angel of men, I here conjure you to bring the truth into this circle as you have done many times before. Here with the blood of this innocent animal your servant I make the dark curtains over my face and over my heart.

(Adept now takes up sword and with a cutting motion at appropriate moments addresses the Magic Theatre.)

O Lucifer, light beyond darkness, I beseech you open the veil so that the light you are will be revealed to this catechumen Matthew now presented to you. By the token of this sword-cut which wounds the dark air I open the night. Open! Open! Open! Open! Open!

(The lights on the Magic Theatre throb as he cries 'Open' and swishes his sword, and then, as if drawn unwilling forth, at a gap in the black curtains like a slash, a white appearance shows, flashing out with each sword-stroke. There steps out of the black a figure dressed in a blazing white hooded monk's garment. The face is invisible.)

As I wound the air with this sword so the veils of illusion part and the bright energy at the roots of existence is revealed to us.

(At this, the hooded figure throws off its robe and reveals a rather horrid and convincing skeleton-suit. With gestures the Spirit-clown-skeleton indicates that there is more to be seen. The Magician stares at the apparition; the Protagonist, who sees none of this, stares at the Magician.)

See there! Is this vision not worth the death of a dog? Now show us, O Life-in-Death, what more there is to see.

(The skeleton detaches one of its legs and we see underneath a neatly-trousered leg, ditto the other. He then detaches his ribby chest, revealing a neat jacket and waistcoat and a bow-tie. The pelvis comes off next, and the rest of the trouser is seen. Then the skull comes off and there is a conventional neat-bearded Mephistopheles-face, such as one might see at a pantomime. The Devil smiles dazzlingly, and then begins to do some banal conjuring-tricks, suitable for a children's party. It then begins to tap-dance. The Adept cannot believe what he sees. Stunned, he walks out of the safety of the circle with incredulous gestures. Clutches heart. Falls to ground. Clown-spirit stops dance, shrugs shoulders, and disappears through black curtain. Lights go out

on Magic Theatre. Protagonist, who has seen only the Adept conjuring and his collapse, is left standing.)

Protagonist: Well, as the lights have gone out, I suppose it is safe to leave the circle.

(Walks over to Adept and feels heart.)

Dead as a doornail. I wonder what he thought he saw. Some demon more overpowering and terrible than even he could suppose. Ah well, I think he strained his capacities. Exit Adept.

(Second Helper-acolyte enters and drags Adept's corpse out. Protagonist walks to side to give acolyte a chance to remove small circle, continues to address audience.)

I did not feel too well myself after that. What the magician saw killed him. I only saw him killed, and that gave me a nasty turn. Would I be pursued by the demonic vision? Would I have to be exorcised? Must I flee to the bosom of Mother Church? I fled to the bosom of my family instead, but the bosom had got a bit lumpy and uncomfortable by that time. Things had become not at all easy back home.

(Walks back into main performance area. Helper as Wife comes to meet him. As she does so, Magic Theatre lights up.)

Wonderful night! Moonlight on the still waters. A bright silver path over the lake, guttering into the black unknown. Get a baby-sitter, let's go out tonight. Get mother-in-law to stay all night. We'll take a room with a bath at the Medusa's Head, get stoned. Wine, spotless tableclothes, hushed service, the glitter of the knives and forks, the black coats of the waiters, their slick black hair.

A bit of wine, silver candlesticks, candlelight. The glittering lake, the back of the car, a night to remember. What about it?

Wife: Get drunk, spend money, screw. If that's your idea of a romantic evening it's not mine. Go out with your spooky friends. Get your table-turners drunk on real spirits for a change. Get your magician-friend to understand the real black magic: moonlight on the deep lake at night.

Protagonist: He's dead. The magician.

Wife: If the magician's dead then the Medium will find him.

Protagonist: Sweetie! It was a genuine offer. OK then, I'll not drink. We'll not touch a drop. You know it's only nerves.

Wife: What are you so worried about all the time? Why don't you try running a household for a bit? If you had nappies to change and wash you'd think a bit less and feel a bit more. Keep your feet on the ground.

Protagonist: I can't stand your endless self-righteousness.

Wife: Women's work and children's play. These are the mysteries.

Protagonist: I don't see anything mysterious about babyshit.

Wife: You would if you had to wait around for the baby when he's constipated.

(Clown-spirit dressed as baby in enormous nappy toddles out on Magic Theatre stage, and crosses footlights on to human acting-area.)

Protagonist: Exactly my point. Women's work and children's play. You're training the baby. This is preparation for common life, not final mysteries.

Wife: You and your final mysteries. What about the mysteries of beginnings.

(Pause.)

Protagonist: Then you'll not come out with me.

Wife: I'll not go out on a drunken binge and spend all that money.

Protagonist: You're a frigid bitch.

(Clown-spirit acts frightened child running to mother and clutching her knees.)

Wife: You come home smelling of drink. You plump down in the chair in front of the television-set with your whisky and go to sleep. You spend no time with the baby, and as for bed, you're never sober. What sort of a life is that for lovers?

Protagonist: If you let your hair down sometimes I'd have something to come home to. There's vision in drink too, you know.

Wife: That's very nice. In front of the child too. Well, I tell you what I'll do tonight. I'll pack. You'll find you've lost your wife, your home and your baby. I'm going to do *my* vanishing trick.

Protagonist: I'll kill you, you bitch!

(Steps toward them, murderous. The lights on the Magic Theatre go out, the Clown-spirit frees himself from the Wife and rushes back under

the black curtains, the Wife rushes off separately. Protagonist is left weeping in the middle of the stage. Pause. Then he crosses downstage to a suitable talking-position.)

>*Occide mulierem.* I could have killed the woman. I nearly did. It would have given me great energy to slaughter her. So the Black Magic Man was right, after all. Pity he had such a weak heart. All this left me in a terrible state. I thought I was being punished for dabbling in magic, for believing in the spirits of the dead. My son was not really all that important to me. I felt so cold deep down that I knew Hell didn't really exist either. Freud was right: it was our repressions that kept us going. My experiences had removed all my inhibitions, so I fell silent. I did however still have some things to tell a psychoanalyst.

(Crosses over from talking-place to performance area. Lies down on recliner-chair for Helper, who enters as Analyst.)

Analyst: Well now, we're quite private in here. You can tell me your troubles. You feel cold, played out. There is nothing that excites you? A dead cinder are you? Too much trouble even to speak, is it? Well, I wonder if we can find what is deep down. Rake over the cinders maybe. So long as you can walk, and talk, there is hope. Let me see whether I can guess what has brought you to this pass. You know, an analyst is supposed to have insight; together we must make the inner lights go up.

(Lights on the Magic Theatre go up.)

>I wonder if I can guess what goes on in your deep mind. I must relax myself for this, and you too must be relaxed. We shall see what we shall see. We must concentrate together.

(A Clown-spirit passes across the magic stage with a cut-out shield. She reverses it suddenly and shows that the back is covered with hair. It is an immense vagina. She waves it around a bit, then goes off.)

> I have read your case-history, which tells me a lot about what you got up to in the past. I know you were very close to your mother. What pictures come into your mind as you think of your mother?

(A Clown-spirit carrying a great penis hurries over the stage in pursuit of the vagina. A large pair of cardboard scissors follows.)

> You say nothing. I wonder if you have any fetishes. You know during these hard times in our lives, we tend to regress. This means that we like childish things. Little sexual experiences we had as a child tend to come back to us but, since we are grown up, carry the power of an adult sexuality.

(One of the Clown-spirits in a nurse-maid's headdress with a large moustache crosses the stage.)

> These images can be very helpful to us, since they carry safely with them our sexual energy, and indulging them can bring the light and purpose back to our lives.

(A number of fetishes walk across the stage using black-theatre techniques. A lovely pair of shiny silk stockings on a suspender-belt walks across in high-heeled shoes. A pair of enormous tits floats past. A strait-jacket, festooned in chains. Protagonist sits up at these and begins talking brightly, looking straight at them.)

Protagonist: Do you know, doctor, I do believe you're right. I used to think of the strangest things when I was a young boy. It's all coming back to me. Bondage. Silk stockings. You know. I wonder if I can remember. I had the strangest fantasy. It was a woman — at least I think it was a woman. She wore a white laboratory coat. She would have intercourse with me in this white laboratory coat. She was a highly-qualified scientist. I could smell the strange exciting chemicals of her work on her skin. She was a chemist. She worked on explosives. She wore her collar high because she was scarred with acid under her clothes. I thought that if I could meet such a woman then I would be complete. I would not see her as ugly. She would not be ignorant and silly like so many of the girls I met. She would have knowledge, and would take control. In turn I would soothe her poor acid-wracked body.

(An empty white coat crosses the stage of the Magic Theatre, teasingly.)

Yes, I can see it now, that consummate relationship. I would transcend the bounds of my ordinary body, I would not be confined by my ordinary sexual being, but I would marry this great woman and be wife to her masculine virtues.

Analyst: I *see*. Your *soror mystica*.

Protagonist: Do you people always have to put things into Latin?

Analyst: Your alchemical companion, your sister of the work. Though she would be more like a brother to you. I have just the thing for you!

(He pulls out a magnificent ball gown and wig for Protagonist and fits it on him; puts one on himself. The second Helper drifts in, magnificently apparelled in drag. The lights of the Magic Theatre are still up, and one of the Clown-spirits also glides in to swell the numbers of the drag party.)

Helper or Spirit: Oh, hello, Ms Matthew. You look lovely tonight. Have you met Gladys? She is a spiritualism medium you know. She has a red guide, haven't you, Gladys?

Helper or Spirit: Actually, my dear, you're days behind. I'm into black magic now. Those sprightly little imps! It was after my analysis, you know. I went in with a stiff collar and a bowler hat and an umbrella.

Protagonist: I know, and you came out looking stunning.

Helper or Spirit: I think you look charming yourself.

Helper or Spirit: Well, that's very nice. But who is this *creature*?

(M's fantasy-figure, the lady-scientist in the white coat, comes from the Magic Theatre, the drag-queens all stand affronted and drift off, leaving Matthew in drag and girl in white coat confronting each other as in wife-scene.)

Spirit: I wish you wouldn't go about like that, even in the house.

Protagonist: Let's go out tonight.

Spirit: One of those candlelight suppers. The light shining over your bare shoulders and setting off your diamonds in your evening gown.

Protagonist: This (looking down) was just an expedient. My psychiatrist told me to . . .

Spirit: Oh, pull the other one. It's got lace on it.

Protagonist: Truly. Let's go out together. Like the old times.

Spirit: Oh light on the lake and all that drag. You ineffably passive and me always having to dress up in this gear.

Protagonist:	I can't stand your endless self-righteousness.
Spirit:	I work all day at the lab to give you a home and . . .
Protagonist:	That's what I mean. I suppose I haven't got feelings. I slave all day over the child and the housework . . . Woman's work and children's play, you know.
Spirit:	This is where I came in.
Protagonist:	Then stuff it.
Spirit:	Right then I will. But not with a drag-queen. Goodbye.
Protagonist:	Don't leave me.

(Spirit in white coat returns to Magic Theatre. Lights go abruptly out. Protagonist tears off his drag costume. Flings his wig away, returns to talking-place.)

Turn and turn about. I was no good as the opposite sex either. That feeling of holiness that gets clergymen into drag didn't work out for me. I was on my own again. What development of feeling, what further stage of quest was left for me now?

(The lights in the Magic Theatre come on.)

Perhaps this was the time for me to sink down into myself, as the Black Magic man said. Surely I am scoured out now, have hung up my hang-ups and can walk away from them.

(Beautiful objects now pass across the black stage, all in white. A procession of bones, antelope skull, nautilus shell, chalk carvings, a beautiful white spangled clown's costume.)

The beautiful images pass through my mind. Perhaps I was always meant to be a poet. Yes, that's it, a poet. If I were a poet, a true one, I would be free of all beliefs, all obsessions, except for the fancies that crossed my mind. If I'm a poet it doesn't matter what I believe! Perhaps this is the only truth: life is a poet's dream. Then I could turn the Magic Theatre on and off as I pleased, and no longer be afraid of ghosts or demons. There! I turn the lights off. There! on they come again.

(Lights in Magic Theatre come on and off at his command.)

I will sit here and see what inspiration brings me. I think I will write a poem about God, a free and beautiful poem because I know that God has no real existence, there is only the magic theatre of the mind, that is alight always when we want it, and only goes dark when we die. Then all is over. Now I will see what inspiration brings me.

(He sits down and watches the stage attentively for what will appear: a large human skull appears on the stage.)

I see the symbol for Death again. That is my subject. I will say 'God says', like they say 'O'Grady says', because then it must be done.

God says 'Death' in a gentle voice

Who would God make that remark to? Why, to the beings that understand it, those who are dead, the corpses.

(A woman crowned with a wheat-sheaf enters.)

God says 'Death' in a gentle voice
To the corpse sleepless with the wheats

(A sound of soughing wind comes through the speakers.)

    That hiss on a low earth-note all night

(The sound of whispered 'Death' comes out of the immense speakers.)

    Like a door hung over with dark leaves
    Out of which the immense syllable blows:

(The dead magician comes in, carrying a green bough.)

    'Death' in God's voice dressed in his spiderweb shirt
    With its tassels of wheat, in his knobbly
                    dressing-gown
    Pulled from the oak; he
    Says 'Death' with all his clothes,

    And his mushroom buttons,
    And his ponds which are mirrors
    Tunnelling into the sky where he jumps up
    Parting the thundercloud with electrical claws;

(Thunder over the soughing through the speakers.)

    The reedy marshes of the railway, on some platform
    Deep in East Anglia with the mire-drummer thumping
    Through the lonely sky, God might pop out of the mud
    Puffing a smoke rolled of flesh, dung and pelt,
    And offer me one

(On Magic Theatre stage, a cloaked man with a big hat, like the Sandeman's port advert, with back to audience.)

    And I could ask him then why 'Death',
    And he would smile like a dago in his black cloak,
    And offer me life to keep quiet about it,

(Figure on Magic Theatre stage wheels to show calmer smiling face. The figure stretches out a hand.)

> 'Would you call God a liar?' he hands me flowers
> From the churchyard: 'Do you call these dead?'

(A second spirit, as if in obedience to the outstretched hand of the first, creeps from the theatre and places a bunch of yellow flowers on the table. Protagonist sees it, and cries out with pleasure.)

Why, an apport! Where do these things come from? 'They are something which just happens. They bring good luck,' said the spiritualist. But can they come from the mind alone? That was my death-poem. It may be beautiful, but it's only poetry, and it's only about God. Can we ever really know what goes on behind the scenes? Is it all mere radiation in a void, like the neutron bomb, emptying a space for itself? I made my death-poem, so now it was time for me to die, and as I died, I saw something, as I told you in the beginning, and I wonder whether it is true.

(He is still on his couch or chair, and we know he is dying. The lights on the Magic Theatre slowly dim, and go out slowly; then a very bright light grows and pours from the theatre straight into the audience's eyes, like a neutron bomb, and this fades, and there is left for us to see, thrown in profile silhouette from behind the scenes, what is truly there, the man spirit and the woman spirit of the Magic Theatre, their profiles moving towards each other and touching with a kiss. Hold. Black out.)

Guy sat with the pages of Matthew's play spread out in front of him. Matthew's last work made him feel hopelessly sad, since his friend seemed to want to die, and die alone, believing in nothing but the possibility of a ghost's kiss. The world was not created by kissing! The play was pure, innocent, and hopeless. Guy wanted to find his friend and take care of him. No good was coming to him at that Institute. Whatever 'phenomena' were occurring there were not fulfilling his friend's life. Would Millie let him live here, in this house? But what was Matthew like, now? Guy had missed him since that first drinkless, dowsing day. It seemed the tides of whisky had receded and left an empty, meatless shell, scoured clean and dead and full of echoes. The phone rang, and Guy noticed that Millie had got up as if to answer it a second or two before the first ring.

II

'Matthew wants to see you, Millie. Can you come over?' Meave's voice was difficult to hear on the phone; it was calling from far away in a sea-foam of static.

'Can't he come to the phone and tell me himself?' Millie hated that Institute; she'd go up if Matthew asked her.

'I'm afraid he can't come to the phone. He's not well.'

'But he was here a moment ago.'

'Was he now?' said Meave's voice with a little tremble in it: Millie thought it might have been fear, or suppressed laughter.

'He's been taken ill and wants to see you.'

'Me, not Guy?'

'No, it's you he wants to see, Millie. Shall I tell him you'll come?'

'Yes, of course' — Millie was now on her mettle — 'just give me a chance to phone for a taxi.'

Meave rang off without another word. Guy looked at Millie reproachfully, as she told him to stay in the house until she called.

When she got to the Institute, Meave opened the door. She stepped forward and silently embraced Millie, who resisted a little to begin with, but felt that Meave was serious now if not on the phone, so she returned the hug. There was still something in the air she didn't like. They went through the gloomy hall (there was a chink of bright light reaching in from the edges of the door of the white room) and climbed up the heavy firm stairs. At the top was a big landing, and the old doctor David was standing at one of the doors. He motioned the two women in, did not come in himself, and shut the door on them. Matthew was lying on the bed, very grey, very still, his eyes closed. He was dressed in a shirt and trousers. There was a pen and some sheets of writing on a table by the bed.

Millie went to the bed quickly and touched his cheek. It was cold and lax. She turned. 'He's dead! Matthew's dead.'

'We found him this morning.'

'Why didn't you tell us at once?' Millie felt the room swimming, and sat down on a chair. Matthew looked as though he were sleeping, except for that greyness, like a light shading of lead pencil. 'Why didn't you ask Guy to come up too!'

'We will, but we wanted to talk to you first. Matthew left you something.'

'Do you mean his play? He gave me that.'

'What play? I mean his child.' Millie could not take in what Meave was saying. 'He is a spirit now, Millie. Spirits must live.'

Millie felt a strong hand gripping her shoulder. When she turned her head she found that Simon was there, and was looking at her with an expression that made her blood tingle. Gently he lifted her to her feet and walked her over to the bed, and tried to sit her down on it, next to Matthew's body. Simon's hand was cupped round her breast. Millie realised that he meant to make love to her on the bed where her dead friend was lying, and she struggled free. Meave was guarding the door. 'Not here!' Millie cried out and Simon lifted her off her feet and carried her swiftly out of the room, into another, with a big dark bed in it. He put her on the bed and lifted her skirt and began kissing her vulva. Millie had had no opportunity to recover from the shock of discovering death, and Simon was playing on this. Death and sex were always linked, and the honest mourner found the funeral sexy. The widow needed to be swived, for her comfort. Millie thought that her love for Matthew had made her go as cold as his skin, but like a little voice distant on the telephone, she felt her tremendous orgasm rushing toward her. There! it had come, and she was threshing in water so sharply cold that it made her cry out. Then the wave ebbed, and she felt like some empty and clean shell left on the shore. This brought to mind the shell of the poet in the next room, and tears came weakly to her eyes.

'Simon . . .' she said and ran her fingers through his hair where he rested, his head against her thigh. 'Simon, I'm so weak . . .'

'Then I'll make you strong, Millie. Take some of my strength.' He slid up from where he was and lay beside her, and put her hand into the opening of his trousers. 'I want you to love me here, Millie, and make me come, and I will show you how you can get strength from that.' He guided her hand to the right place, and began fitting it and kneading it round himself. Her hand took life and worked on him, and he began to groan and sigh. His climax came quickly, and he leaned forward with his mouth open and breathed into her mouth as it did so. She took the full breath in, as she was breathing rapidly in excitement, and there was a tang in it, like spindrift, like breeze off the sea. Clarity began to come back into her mind, and she raised herself on her elbows to try and take stock of where she was, but, incredibly, he was hard again, and had her further thigh between his legs, so that they lay at right-angles, and he penetrated her as with his hand he rubbed her clitoris. Once again her climax came; she realised it had never gone but had been hovering all the time — like a spirit she thought — but this time it was like fire kindled low down in the hearth of her body and rising upwards through it, like flames roaring upwards in a chimney. She felt the heat and saw the light of these flames, but they were like an inflammable liquid thrown into the fire; after the explosion they died away leaving something very like cold and disappointment.

Millie moaned. At the further end of the room, shadows stirred. David got up from the chair where he had been sitting. He had a glass in his hand of dark liquid. 'Drink this, Millie'; he raised her head. The liquid slid down warming her as it went, and she slept.

David had a comfortable consulting-room on the ground floor, and it was here that Guy was invited when he arrived, hot and furious, in the early morning. Meave, not Millie, had called him up, but she had been persuasively reassuring. Now David broke the news, and told him of the death. Guy sat down suddenly, and forgot his rage. His first reaction was that he wanted to see his friend. David told him that that would not be possible until just before the funeral, as Matthew had already been taken away.

'Who signed the death certificate?'

'I did,' said David.

Guy wanted to know how Matthew had died. David put on his blandest consultant's manner for this, and said that he was afraid that Matthew had gone back on the drink, and a brain artery had ruptured: it was a stroke.

'Why did he go back to drink? What about your treatment; wasn't it going much better than anybody had expected?' Guy's eyes ran along the comforting rows of bound psychological journals.

'I wouldn't have called it "treatment" exactly,' said David; 'it was self-development in the strictest sense. We have found, you see, that people drink because they have impulses in them to which neither they nor society can give a name. A man may drink to forget or conceal or substitute for a sexual preference that seems disreputable, and he may do this for many years.' David's white, carefully-combed hair looked as sleek as spun sugar. 'In due time, the drink loses its efficacy, so he takes more. It's a moot point whether the drink or the suppressed desires kill him.'

'Matthew had no kinks like that, did he? He was surely slightly undersexed, if anything.'

'No, I don't think so, nor do I subscribe to the idea of undersexed or oversexed. You should talk to Meave about Matthew's sex-life.'

Guy promised himself this doubtful pleasure. 'But in a man of that age . . .'

'Do you think people age when they are doing what they need to do in life? Would you say I was old?'

Guy looked at David, at the white hair, and the skin that looked quite transparent and young, rather like Simon's. 'I should say that you are in your late sixties.'

David opened a drawer in his desk. 'I keep a copy of this here and wherever I treat patients. I find it a help to be a good advertisement for my own psychology.' He slid across the desk the red form of a birth certificate. Guy looked at it: David's full name was written there and he saw that he had been born on 4 September 1889.

'That makes you ninety-one!' Guy said. 'Is this yours?'

'Do you doubt me?' asked David.

'No, not really. Do you expect to live to be a hundred?'

'Whenever I die, I shall simply leave this shell sitting here. It is like a statue of David, and I am looking at you through this statue's eyes. I shall one day be tired of this container and walk away from it. I am strong and fit, and there is no reason why I should not die as a person should, having decided to die.'

'But poor Matthew.'

'Yes, I'm afraid he came to this work rather late, and his nerves were frayed. As I was telling you, the desire to drink conceals unacknowledged powers that the subject wishes to hide away from himself. We gave them a name for Matthew . . .

'You told him he was a medium of spooks, when he was a fine poet!'

'Guy! you should talk! We know all about your experiments in this kind of thing with Millie. That is why we want you to join us.'

'Where is Millie?' asked Guy, rising.

'Let me finish, please. Matthew was a fine — let us say, medium — and the spirits talked very clearly through him. It was a development of his powers as a poet. Yet he was too fixed in his habits of mind, and expected the spirits always to be truthful, as, he said, poetry is: if it were not, the language would not get up and walk about — those were his words. But there are playful or lying spirits, that catch on to one's deepest fears, and sometimes one is several spirits oneself, and one cannot tell the hosts from the guests.'

'This is what happened to Matthew.'

'Certainly. He obtained a remarkable communication from a very powerful spirit who was fixed in her moment of death. He wanted to release her by incarnation. We have methods of doing this.'

'What methods?'

'Would you like to know? You and Millie would be welcome to join us.'

'What methods?' asked Guy again. 'Have you successfully performed any experiment?' His tears for his friend began to rise.

'We have, Guy, but until you've been with us for a while I can't expect you to understand or believe.'

'Who are Simon and Meave? Your friends, assistants?' Understanding began to dawn. 'Are Simon and Meave your son and daughter?'

'You're warm, Guy . . .' — a beautiful smile grew on David's face 'they are my twins, but there's something more . . .'

'I'd really like to hear more about Matthew.'

'It was an exceedingly important document that he gave us, and it has been lost!' David exploded.

'What, do you mean his play?'

'I know of no play. This was a communication that revealed a political plot!'

'What sort of a plot?'

David seemed to feel that he had said too much. 'A search is being made . . .' he rumbled; 'but haven't you guessed yet, Guy, about us? Let me tell you. Simon and I made Meave's twins between us. We're her lovers, both of us. I want you, and Simon and me, to make Matthew again by loving Meave; and he will be twins then; because when my father died, I made him again, with my mother, and he was the twins you call Meave and Simon . . .'

Guy's manual of sex-magic had not prepared him for anything like this. 'David, if you don't mind, I want to talk all this over with Millie. It has been a terrible shock, and, as for joining you, I really don't know if you are not rather advanced for us, to say the least. I have my friend's death to think about, and that is too much for me already.'

'But his spirit is lingering,' screamed David, half-rising; 'even now it hovers just beneath the ground, shackled to the water, and unless we give him a face again, the water will run away with him.'

'I'm sorry, David, I just can't take this.' Guy was near the door now. 'I'm very sorry. .

'If you leave us now, you can take our curse with you.' David had completely altered. His eyes were bolting out of his head and his mouth was turned down like a Javanese mask, he was leaning forward with his knuckles on the desk and stood as though he was shouting silently.

Guy then did the bravest thing he could remember. He went back to the desk and stood in front of the furious old man. 'David,' he said quietly, 'I have every respect for you and confidence in you, and I will, upon my solemn oath, keep your secrets. I will even work with you when I have studied sufficiently, though I don't believe either Millie or myself could join your community. Let me be, just for now; and I ask you, out of the respect which I already have for you, do not, please, excite yourself in this manner, as, though I am no doctor, I can see that it will bring your great work to an end before it is ready.'

'Thank you, Guy,' said David, sinking back into his seat again, 'but you know nothing about our training if you imagine I was angry. There is calm within, you know, and a strength coiled to strike, behind the faces of the deliberately wrathful. You must know that Millie has already become a member, so you might as well join yourself.'

Chapter five

The lighted doors

I

Guy and Millie, like so many of us, were scarcely able to assimilate their own immediate troubles, let alone feel and understand those of the larger world. National news was bad all over. The country's inflation galloped, and there seemed no way out of the old spiral that the more one earned, the less it bought. Freelance literary work was in a particularly bad way: fees for reviewing and the like had not kept pace with modern life: the rates seemed fixed back in the 1950s. Guy did not earn the £10,000 a year that made it compulsory for people to register for VAT, and though it was not worth his while to do so and recover the tax he still felt in all sorts of marginal ways the added impost that VAT had brought into day-to-day life. Hotel bills and travelling had gone up. It was as though, with decimalisation and VAT, some concealed blow had been struck at the living of self-employed people. The world's money-markets had gone crazy, and it gave no comfort to see that Marx was right after all, and they were witnessing the break-up of the Western capitalistic system. The world's reaction to the fever in its fiscal networks was irrationally hectic, as if to assist the crash: one could not open the paper without reading about hijacking of aeroplanes and kidnappings of rich infants. In London itself, the police had concluded that there was a bomb-factory — perhaps working for the Palestinians, perhaps for the Irish — perhaps for neither, but simply hiring out their services. A London bus had been burnt out by a bomb planted on the lower deck: most of the passengers had been able to get out of the emergency exits, but the bomb itself exploded in the face of a queue of people who were just getting on, laden with shopping, in Oxford Street. Five died. A hotel was bombed, and a news photographer who happened to be on the spot snapped a famous picture of a policeman weeping at the carnage: posh clientele and liveried servants were as one in the wrecked lobby. Another much-published photo showed a woman in the rags of an ermine jacket cradling in her arms a bleeding desk-clerk. Plutonium was found in the lungs of workers at an atomic rescarch plant, which was under the strictest security precautions against the escape of radioactive contamination, and this made it extremely unlikely that anyone would accept the assurances of the authorities on atomic energy that the proposed nuclear power-stations were anything but a terrible hazard: either from leakage of used but deadly radioactive fuel, or from its being stolen by terrorists to create home-made nuclear devices. But the facts would not affect the decisions; it seemed that these two had for ever parted company. Experimental virus escaped from a secure microbiological research unit, and Great Britain was declared a smallpox area, so that all travellers were obliged to get a certificate of vaccination before going anywhere abroad. Botulism had been found in the fish tinned by a famous firm.

After his disturbing interview with David, Guy had found Millie waiting for him in the hall of the Institute. She was on her own, and Guy was glad to find this; having just avoided a scene with David, he didn't want to have to fight to retrieve Millie. She looked crumpled and shaken-up. She was morose, and at first wouldn't speak to him. When they got home she went silently into the kitchen and got him some scrambled eggs. They ate together without talking. Guy went and put on some coffee and came back to the table. 'What awful people,' he said. Millie was weeping. 'Millie, what is it?' He went and held her, which she took quite passively, her body shaking with the sobs. He took out his hankie and wiped her face, but she flinched away. 'Guy . . . please let me alone. Give me an aspirin and let me go to bed.' He got her the aspirin from the kitchen cupboard, and she washed it down with coffee. Then, without looking at him, she went upstairs. A little while later she was calling out. She met him at the top of the stairs, and kissed him. 'Dear Guy, it's all right — look.' He was surprised at what she showed him: she held out her pants, and he saw blood marking them. Her period was not a thing she usually bothered about, though they were not looking to have a child and they were quite glad when it came. She had given up the Pill and used a diaphragm now, or nothing at all when she was actually bleeding. 'Come to bed with me, Guy. I want to celebrate getting away from those people.' They undressed, both of them feeling their pleasure in each other beginning to mount, a very much better end to the day than they had expected. Guy, after the intensities of the morning, wanted to lie still, and let Millie make love to him: her recesses were very warm and caressing. As he was going off to sleep he had a quick vision or 'flash' of Matthew climbing some stairs, his back to him.

He woke to bright sunlight and was amazed to find that it was nearly midday. He got dressed and made a cup of tea and started up an early lunch, leaving Millie sleeping. He found various papers rather prominent in the untidy living-room: there were the two big scrolls of his and Matthew's automatic writing, which he slid into elastic bands and put away out of sight on the top of the bookcase. There were others in the chest under the window, but this was nearly full. Matthew's play was scattered on the table and he tidied this away in the drawer. He wanted to find out from the Institute when the funeral was, and where, but was in great conflict, for he felt that he and Millie had escaped a danger, and he did not want to go back into it, even by way of the telephone. The newspaper was on the floor, and as he picked it up two items caught his attention. One was the announcement of a choirs festival in the town. He had a sudden feeling that he might like to go, and take Millie; it was such a disinterested business, choir-singing; complicated and skilful, and performed for its own sake; quite as magical as anything *they* had been doing, with the dead composers living again in their songs, and the little angel voices of the children, clean as ghosts, all dressed in identical spiritual uniforms, with strange spirit clothes of ruff and surplice: fashions of a bygone time refleshed. The other item was a very curious explosion in a supermarket: a bomb had gone off during the night when there were no shoppers in the store and the reporter said that the pyramids of tinned food had been affected in a curious way by the bomb-blast. Food had been blown right out of the tins without disturbing their arrangements on the shelves: dog-meat, corned beef, pie-fillings, sweetcorn and ready-made custard had been crushed into a great pile at one end of the store, and the firemen had dug it out with shovels. Guy took her tea up to Millie, and when he came down again, took a pad to the seance-table and wrote a poem, the first since he and Matthew had taken up dowsing. In his mind he dedicated the poem to his friend.

THE BOMBS

Glistening marrow into glowing wheat
A great cellar full of blood-coloured cobwebs

His tears ran down his legs
He was unable to cross the road for the weeping people

The bomb exploded in the supermarket
No one was hurt. All the food

Was blown out of the cans in a glistening mess
All the tins quite empty on their shelves, rocking.

The other bomb went off during choir practice
In the church and everybody was hurt

Many will not sing again after that shout
I could not cross the road for weeping people

One woman saying over and over
Jesus has been here to lead the innocents home

Jesus has been here to lead the innocents home
There were bloody footsteps in the chancel

Blood and brains in the lap of the Virgin
The small cakes of Jesus ground into the fireman's water

The stone tombs stained but quite dry
As though they had drunk thirstily

The face blown off one boy, his raw skull
Glistened above the crisp ruffles of surplice

Gristle in the pulpit, a large piece
Stuck on the wooden desk where the bible had been

None of the stained glass had been broken
Though the great doors were off in the West

The unruffled saints glowed below the glass crucifixion
Jesus stepped out of his tomb just beyond the surface

I wanted innocents trooping into the picture
Identical naked children stripped of their flesh

Stripped of their bones, but the choir stalls
Were packed full with the lips and the bones

The headlong organist was buried in his machine
They scrubbed the church but it should not have been
                    touched

It should have been left corrupting
With the good flies and their worms busy as a
                    congregation

Of the people in a flash turned to torn bread for them
As a picture-sight for the times

Photographed, and sold on railway stations
At all the resorts to flavour the holiday seaside

Says Seamus, to flavour the ice-creams and innocent
                    lemonade;
A perfume bottled and sold called Reek of the Innocents

One dab behind the ear creates a deathshead.

Guy became absorbed in drafting his poem. He wrote a second long-hand version, then unzipped the portable and typed it out with a carbon copy. He went out to turn the potatoes down, then had another look at the work. It seemed all right to him, and he remembered that he had promised a poem to a journal called *Peacework*. He thought this might be the one for them, so he scribbled a note and put the pages into an envelope, which he stamped. He thought he would go out and post it now, so it would catch the lunchtime van. He called out to Millie, and carefully shut the front door. It took ten minutes to the post office. By the time he got back, the meat would be ready and he could carve it and take it up to Millie, who still had not told him exactly what had taken place at the Institute, but he thought it must have been quite tough going. He himself felt that he had confronted a human bomb, when he remembered David's real or pretended anger in his consulting-room. The man was buzzing like an angry bee, he thought, a white-haired bee, an old queen who wanted to rule all the hive and all the generations himself. After writing the poem Guy felt a good deal saner. He found he could play with the events that had shocked him so, he was not drawn into them, he was a player and not a pawn. He remembered *The Holy Sinner* — Thomas Mann's odd novel — concerning a man who had a son by his sister, and who was therefore both father and uncle to the boy. The boy's mother was his aunt too, and he was, of course, nephew to his father and his mother. Then this son years later met up with his mother, with whom he had children. These children were the cousins of the son-father, and his parents therefore were both grandmother and grandfather, great-uncle and great-aunt. Since the children were cousins, they might inter-marry, so they would have offspring who were nephews and nieces too, but in addition first and second cousins. Guy was able to reel all this off in his mind because he had once done a radio version of *The Holy Sinner* for the BBC. The son of the siblings, who had inadvertently committed these incestuous crimes, was Gregory the Great. The core of his sin was becoming related to himself, which was the prerogative of gods — who were always impregnating virgins in order to beget themselves, thus becoming their own fathers by their own daughters. Gregory had to prove how holy he was by undergoing terrible ordeals, the worst of which was to be confined to a pinnacle of rock for eighteen years, so that he shrank to the size of a hedgehog. He was rescued from this by the Curia of Rome, who had had a dream of where the new Pope was to be found, and came to rescue him, but could not believe that this straggly hedgepig or rockpig was their new Papa. But they did, and he prayed, and repented, and did such good works and became so holy that he was at last able to confess his mother-wife-aunt.

David was evidently in this situation: self-inflated to godhood, and had trapped poor Matthew by the half-health of his studies. What a poison the man was! A bomb pretending to be an alchemist's stone, that truly would transform everything by tearing it to pieces, like that bomb in the church of his poem. Poems help in unexpected ways: the oddities of horror in his had cleared his mind. Perhaps, Guy thought, as he slipped the letter in the box and waved to the postmistress through the window of the small sweetshop-cum-sub-post-office, he should have sung instead of swarms of bees replacing shattered stained glass parables with tall golden honeycomb, turning the terrible carnage by incessant labour into sweetness and light. That would have been far too unrealistic, he felt as he retraced his steps. We have our private magic and our own dead, and if Millie and I are innocent in some ways, we must not corrupt that desirable state by projecting all our disagreeable feelings conveniently away from ourselves on to David. Matthew is, was, a grown man, able to take his own decisions, and if I, Guy, am jealous that he went away to the other camp, then that jealousy is also a part of love, a chewy, indigestible part, but meat of love nevertheless, and full of nourishment if one had the strength of jaw to chew it well. That meat-imagery displeased him; there were very unpleasant under-currents in his apparently happier mind now, and the poem, which was very violent, had not completely dealt with these. Should he brave the Institute and try to find out about the funeral? Probably he would; he had written a poem that was half-way decent and what had David created but misery and lubricity?

Thinking these half-way-happy thoughts, Guy, surprised that the front door was off the latch, stepped into his living-room to find it ransacked, its contents scattered and windows broken as though by a bomb. In the kitchen, the roast was still happily basting and the peas and potatoes simmering, but the living-room was disorder itself. Even the carpet had been ripped up and a bottle of ink had been smashed across the unpainted floorboards. The contents of the sideboard had been pulled out, and a pile of old 78 records lay in jagged black fragments. The lid of the chest in which he had kept his spirit-communications was pulled off its hinges, and the papers had been trodden — he unrolled several and on all of them he found footmarks. Later he realised that whoever it was had pinned the large sheets to the floor with his foot while he pulled them out straight to scan their contents. Matthew's play had been scrutinised and flung into a corner. The few wallet-files of papers Guy kept downstairs were badly treated: they had been torn open and thrown into a heap in the same corner where the burglar had smashed the big flower-vases full of water. The mantelpiece had been swept clean of its clock and its mementoes, which lay shattered on the floor. Carefully placed in the mantelpiece centre was a large black-edged envelope. Looking at it, Guy knew that it was his invitation to Matthew's funeral. But where was Millie? He ran upstairs to find a different sort of disorder. Her clothes were everywhere and a suitcase was missing. It was simply the mess somebody made when they were packing in a hurry to go away. Shoes, some dresses and a suit, presumably underwear, a couple of blouses and the like, and certainly her toothbrush, and diaphragm, had gone. But who had ransacked the living-room, and had Millie gone willingly? Guy was afraid she had, and a sudden picture of big-jawed Simon, so slim and woman-skinned, came into his mind. He went slowly downstairs, got on a chair and looked on the top of the bookcase for the two separately completed scripts of the mad bomber communication. They were still there, tightly rolled up. Guy knew that this was what the burglar had been after. He wondered why. Then he began wondering how he was going to tell his story to the police.

'How long has this woman lived here?' The inspector was very gruff about Guy and Millie not being married.

'We've been together nearly four years. This is not the kind of set-up where a call-girl turns over an apartment after a one-night stand, officer.'

'Oh, you seem to know a lot about that kind of thing, sir.' Guy had given the inspector an opening.

'I'm sorry, no I don't. I am a perfectly respectable householder and rate-payer and I happen to believe, as my partner does, that the marriage contract is degrading both to the woman, and to the man. We prefer to live together without a contract, but we do not force our ideas upon people who wish to take explicit vows. I would be obliged if you did not conclude that we are members of the criminal class, if there is such a thing, because we do not follow your own mode of life. We have broken no law.'

'I'm not married, sir.'

'Then neither of us has broken the law.'

The inspector looked very cross. Guy saw that he must stop condescending, speak to this man professionally like a lawyer or a doctor and not a flunkey. The inspector was intelligent enough to see that Guy meant to imply that a bachelor might be sleeping around — or if not, why not.

Simultaneously the inspector, who was dressed like a country solicitor, in tweeds, relaxed and spoke more openly. It was a danger-sign, if Guy had but known it, and this a policeman of the true sort, a kind of hound, an intuitive who was at the same time down to earth, whose nose once it got the scent would follow it without raising his gaze for a moment, a hunting-machine programmed with a sophisticated code of criminal law. The look of a lawyer he had from his good figure and the tailor of a rich bookie he had once not put away; the professional look meant nothing. Underneath he was sheer hound.

'Well, sir, this is a difficult one. Here is a burglary and a desertion. The desertion may be an absconding too, and the burglary could be an abduction, though I'm inclined not to believe this, as there's no sign of a struggle. On the other hand, valuables have been left untouched; there's a cheque-book and a bank-card and fifteen pounds in cash here, in this drawer. The plywood of the drawer has been smashed, apparently by a beefy fist (which is why I didn't think the lady absconded in the first place) but the useful funds have been left. Your bank account could have been cleared out by now — he could have gone round to any number of branches, cashing fifty pounds each time, and your lady's copperplate signature is not all that difficult to copy. By the same token, if she was not in some way forced to go, why didn't she take her funds? The sergeant has just confirmed to me that there was a burglar — unless you did it yourself, sir, and made away somehow with the lady, which is our third possibility — since somebody has stepped on those curious large writings of yours to pull them out and read them more easily, and left the mark of a fairly slender but not a lady's shoe. To make the whole thing a good deal more uncertain in my mind, you seem to be running some kind of fortune-telling parlour here' — the sergeant had discovered the crystal ball and the planchette, both of which were undamaged — 'and that is rather like a betting-shop in several ways, including the habit of unsavoury characters haunting such places. So you can understand my doubts, can't you, sir, especially as I have a hunch that there's more here than meets the eye, as chaps like us are fond of saying.'

Guy sat down. He saw that he would either have to send the police away, or tell the entire story. Not that he was sure the inspector would listen to it. It had been pointed out to him that if the burglar had come in after the lady had quitted the place, leaving the front door open, then it was not a burglary at all, but a much more minor affair: entering, but not breaking into, enclosed premises. He felt there was much more to it than met his eyes too, nor was it on the level of clairvoyant mysticism either. From the police point of view — perhaps from his own — all that was a trivial business: even poor Matthew's death which, once properly certified by a doctor, had been his own affair. But something prodded him to tell, something quite deep. He thought to himself, would Matthew tell? and he got a sudden Groucho flash behind spectacles from deep inside, and a gesture which dismissed the question as too obvious for reply; and he thought,

Matthew would have spun the police the entire tale, and more, much more besides. He would have loved to put this Inspector Hound with his ratter's jaws on a trail that he could not (by the nature of the beast) relinquish until the whole cast-list had been thoroughly shaken-up — and damn the consequences. He would have loved to tinge, subtly, fact with fiction, to make a bizarre and surrealistic concoction that would exasperate unendurably the official mind with its hints of mysticism and clairvoyance and the odd doings of two suspicious old characters who called themselves poets. 'And serve them all right . . .' he heard faintly and far away, somewhere.

'Inspector. Will you sit down, please. I have a long and rather complicated tale to tell you. It involves a death, which I think you should investigate; and a document which is an original copyright story that I was writing by a rather unusual means with a friend. It is because of this that the lady I live with has left me; and the document that I believe she and her lover were seeking was concealed by me behind the high ornamental front of this bookcase here. It is these papers.'

Guy got on his chair and fished out the papers. Some devilment smoking a big cigar through a greasepaint moustache, walking with its back bent parallel with the ground and its bottom stuck out roguishly, made him embroider still more, made him discard all caution. 'You see, inspector' — this scene would go into his next play, he thought, as he clutched the rolled papers to himself; the inspector having stretched his hand out for them had been baulked by Guy's pulling them back and talking on, still standing on his chair — 'my friend and I believed that we had discovered a terrorist conspiracy run under the front of a respectable Institute of medicine and research' — this will get them into particularly hot water, Guy thought, and as he did so he knew where Millie was and was sure in his bones of what she had been doing, and he felt sweet revenge: the best he could do, anyway — 'but we were afraid for our lives if we went to the police, so we decided to publish our evidence in fictional form. You will be able to check up with other police-forces the details of the characters of known terrorists we have given in our story; all that is missing is the master-plan itself which we have not yet had the time to include — indeed, being interrupted by my dear friend's death. I believe that he was killed in the attempt to force from him a promise of silence . . .' which they obtained, alas, alas. The inspector reached for the scrolls of paper once more, but Guy had not finished. 'The master-plan itself of the Institute was to utilise the public demand for religion and supernatural spectacle by training up accomplished performers at mediumship who, all innocent, would believe that they were inspired. This dastardly band would cause their movement to gather momentum until the public believed that they had a saint and saviour in their midst, and then at a great rally that was planned in the Albert Hall they would explode their largest bomb and blow everybody into the spirit-world. The outcry would be enormous, and there would be immediately declared martial law, and the government would be replaced by a military junta.' Guy sank his voice to a whisper and made his eyes glare. *'The Institute was funded by an extreme right-wing political party that hoped to take over the entire country,'* he hissed, 'and my brave friend had offered himself to the Institute to be trained as their Saint.' The inspector grabbed the papers and began reading them. Guy leaned back in his chair feeling a bit faint; he had hardly known what he was saying, and it seemed to him that he was playing this extravagant trick not only in Matthew's memory, but that somehow Matthew was doing it through him. Guy's pulse was pounding and he was wet with sweat as he had been when he had written his half of the mad bomber communication. But how shall we tell the dead from our imaginations of them?

He looked up. The inspector was hurrying from the room. The sergeant bent down and said something to him which Guy didn't catch, and then left after his inspector. Guy heard the front door close. He went to the mantelpiece, took the card down, and saw that the funeral was at six-thirty that evening. He looked at his watch: he could get a taxi and be there before it was over.

Matthew's funeral was nearly over when he got to the great cemetery on the north road. The taxi had made good time through the homeward-bound traffic, but it was twenty to seven before Guy drew up at the big white gates with the cypress and pine avenues stretching beyond. This was a cemetery on the grand scale; when the town had been wealthy the local mill-owners had continued their fight of keeping up with the Joneses beyond death, and the great carved marble mausolea were a consequence of that fantasy, as though the dead's happiness was to be sealed within elaborate castles and villas of Italian marble guarded by sorrowing angels, as the Muslim heaven is said to be sealed within a pearl. Ranks of white buildings, rather resembling in their style solid plaster-casts of the interiors of saloon bars, stretched away into the distance, under the black fronds, and Guy's footsteps were silenced by fallen needles. He still felt shaky, and he cast a longing eye back at the enormous hotel or, rather, hostelry, that had been built near the gates of the burial ground, to accommodate the living in elaborate refreshments after funeral services. This public house still did a thriving trade, but principally to road-traffic. The magnificent rooms had been conflated into one enormous bar full of crystal and mirror and polished mahogany and wrought iron that, despite the drink and driving restrictions, would be packed out even now, so early. Later on the restaurants on the second and third floors would be similarly full.

But Guy, he remembered just in time, had given up drinking, and he was to go to his friend's funeral sober. Here it was quiet, which the pub was not, and the white fantasies stretched away like blanched inside-out images of pub decoration down to the lower, poorer slopes where the map on the funeral card informed him his friend would be buried. 'Grief, at six-thirty sharp,' said Guy to himself.

As he came out of the cypress shade he saw in the distance, among a myriad white markers, a little black-clothed band of people standing around a parson who had an open book in his hand. Guy hurried down the hill towards them, darting among the tombs, picking his way to and fro, in a kind of crouched alert trot, not at all unlike Groucho hurrying, he felt. There was tall old David, his hair combed sleek as the lines in the parson's open gospel, which was slowly closing as the last words were uttered and Guy came up to the place. Yes, there was Millie, arm in arm with that odious woman-faced Simon, and she looked up and saw Guy, and withdrew her arm. She was in the black suit that had been missing from her bedroom. Simon looked up too, and gave Guy a smile from big teeth, before zipping up his lips again in the irritating half-smile that he usually wore. Meave he could not see; but there were two adolescent children there, also dressed in black; and one or two other people he did not know who he assumed also came from the Institute. Everyone was carrying flowers. The splashes of colour against the black of their coats made Guy weep suddenly, and he brushed his tears away; he wished that he had brought flowers. The parson stared off into the middle distance, praying perhaps, perhaps waiting for everyone to throw their flowers into the big black hole that yawned beneath their feet, and have done. A man had gone down into that hole, as all the many millions had before him, a poet, and there were few enough of those. Millie caught Guy's eyes as he lifted them again, and she stepped round the grave towards him, and touched him lightly on the shoulder, and gave him her flowers. The two were now standing on the other side of the grave from the rest of the party, who seemed to be waiting for the next move. Guy smelt the breath of the anemones in his hand, stepped to the edge of the trench in which Matthew was lying in his big box, and threw his flowers in. He was surprised and pleased to see that the coffin was already covered thickly with flowers: iris and daffodil. His own anemones landed softly on them, without sound. The blaze of colour and scent struck upwards from the grave. David was the next to throw his bouquet in, and just as he did so a bee, that had been foraging in the bunch, plucked free with a zizz. David swiped at it with the slow petulance of an old man as it buzzed on its way. Simon threw his flowers in, looking at Millie. The parson made a gesture to two men who were finishing their tea out of a thermos behind a nearby stone: they were the people who would fill in the grave when the funeral party was gone. Millie said,

'Guy, I've a lot to explain to you. But it's Matthew's festival now. We're all going to the pub to have the kind of party he would have enjoyed, among all the people, at its most crowded and jolly time, just as he would have liked it. I reckon there will be upwards of five hundred people there, and they won't know why we're jolly, but they'll all be drinking to Matthew, even if they don't know it.' Guy thought this was vulgar and sentimental of Millie, especially as Matthew had had his stroke after going back on the bottle. He would rather have been left alone with her among all the ghosts of hostelry architecture that surrounded them, which were at least silent if not sincere. He supposed it would be all right to have a drink to Matthew on this never-to-be-repeated occasion — and then, of course, there was the sweet revenge of his practical joke on these abominable people, whom he could watch revelling in their ignorance while the inspector digested his information and prepared to pounce. So he squeezed Millie's hand and smiled into her eyes, and went and shook hands with David, and with Simon, and the twins, smiling wolfishly like Groucho's Dr Hackenbush, or Rufus T. Firefly, shyster lawyer. He would reserve the wisecracks though.

They toiled up the slope, talking pleasantly but sadly, as befitted a funeral, and the men behind them began filling in Matthew's grave. At the gates they could see the great pub shining all golden and four-square and pinnacled like the city of Jerusalem in a Victorian painter's fantasy. It was barely a hundred yards away, and Guy and Millie lingered behind to let the others go ahead so that Guy could give Millie a quick kiss on the cheek. He was feeling ashamed now of his anger and the joke he had played. They would both have some explaining to do, and the forgiving could be enjoyed too. David's tall back disappeared into the lighted swinging doors of the saloon bars, and Guy held them open for Millie. As he did so he heard a little high buzz like a bee's deep in his ear, and a voice that he recognised said small but quite clearly, 'Christ, boy, I thought you'd given up drinking.' He looked into the pub and saw Meave sitting on a red banquette in front of a table. Simon was just sitting down next to her. She turned her head and saw Guy, and her glance went down to the haversack by her side, on which was stencilled in big faded letters the name 'Sean'. Guy turned back to Millie and let the door go and shouted out to her 'RUN!' and ran to her himself and caught her round the waist and threw her to the ground and into a small sheltering hollow through which a little stream ran as the night blossomed in honey-coloured flame, and blood and glass flew humming and stinging through the night.

Printed in the United Kingdom
by Lightning Source UK Ltd.
134127UK00001B/28/A